Las Vegas College

Classic English Poetry

Being a Collection of Shorter Classic Poems, from Chaucer to Tennyson

Las Vegas College

Classic English Poetry
Being a Collection of Shorter Classic Poems, from Chaucer to Tennyson

ISBN/EAN: 9783744764940

Printed in Europe, USA, Canada, Australia, Japan

Cover: Foto ©Andreas Hilbeck / pixelio.de

More available books at **www.hansebooks.com**

A. M. D. G

CLASSIC ENGLISH POETRY,

BEING

A COLLECTION OF SHORTER CLASSIC POEMS,

FROM CHAUCER TO TENNYSON.

> Jewels five-words long
> That on the stretched fore-finger of all Time
> Sparkle forever.
> TENNYSON.—*The Princess.*

LAS VEGAS COLLEGE,
Las Vegas, New Mexico.

COLLEGE PRESS.

1884.

PREFACE.

Collections of poems are already so many that for adding one more however unpretending—to the number—a word of explanation seems necessary. The present one is intended to supply a want in colleges and schools which could not well be supplied by the larger anthologies: and herein lies its only apology for existence.

A collection of the shorter masterpieces of classic poetry is certainly needed which will serve for the double purpose of illustrating the style of the master-poets in their lesser flights, and of furnishing poems to be committed to memory which are altogether unobjectionable in matter and manner.

For this, the admirable volumes already before the public are hardly suitable: they are all too costly and too unwieldy to be used as class-books; besides which, they contain a great deal of matter that would be somewhat out of place in text-books for the young. To avoid these—in this case—undesirable qualities of costliness and bulk and inappropriate subject-matter has been the aim of the compiler.

He has endeavoured to present in a convenient shape a collection of poems—the choicest of the best—that will be found amply sufficient for the purposes indicated above. And therefore, he has attended more especially to the quality of the poems introduced than to their number, admitting only those that are as free from objectionable modes of thought and expression as from the sin of mediocrity; so that they may be as little prejudicial to the morals of young pupils as to their nascent literary taste.

Las Vegas College,
  May 1, 1884.

CONTENTS.

➤✳THE✛PIPER✳◄

Piping down the valleys wild,
Piping songs of pleasant glee,
On a cloud I saw a child,
And he laughing said to me: —

" Pipe a song about a lamb; "
So I piped with merry cheer.
" Piper, pipe that song again : "
So I piped he wept to hear.

" Drop thy pipe, thy happy pipe "
Sing thy songs of happy cheer ; "
So I sang the same again,
While he wept with joy to hear.

"Piper, sit thee down and write
In a book that all may read— "
So he vanished from my sight;
And I plucked a hollow reed.

And I made a rural pen,
And I stained the water clear,
And I wrote my happy songs
Every child may joy to hear.

WILLIAM BLAKE

·A·SONG·FOR·ST·CECILIA'S·DAY·
→❉1687❉←

From harmony, from heavenly harmony,
  This universal frame began;
When nature underneath a heap
    Of jarring atoms lay,
  And would not have her head,
The tuneful voice was heard from high,
    Arise, ye more than dead!
Then cold and hot, and moist and dry,
  In order to their stations leap,
    And Music's power obey.
From harmony, from heavenly harmony,
  This universal frame began:
  From harmony to harmony,
Through all the compass of the notes it ran
  The diapason closing full in man.

What passion cannot Music raise and quell!
    When Jubal struck the chorded shell,
  His listening brethren stood around,
    And, wondering, on their faces fell,
  To worship that celestial sound.
Less than a God they thought there could not dwell
    Within the hollow of that shell,
    That spoke so sweetly and so well.
What passions cannot Music raise and quell?
    The trumpets loud clangor
      Excites us to arms,
    With shrill notes of anger,
    And mortal alarms.
  The double double double beat
    Of the thundering drum
    Cries, Hark! the foes come;
Charge, charge, 'tis too late to retreat!

The soft complaining flute
  In dying notes discovers
  The woes of helpless lovers.
Those dirge is whispered by the warbling lute.
  Sharp violins proclaim
Their jealous pangs, and desperation,
Fury, frantic, indignation,
Depth of pains, and height of passsion
  Foe the fair, disdainful dame.
  But O, what art can teach,
    What human voice can reach,
  The sacred organ's praise?
    Notes inspiring holy love,
Notes that wing their heavenly ways
    To mend the choirs above.

Orpheus could lead the savage race;
And trees uprooted left their place,
    Sequacious of the lyre,
But bright Cecilia raised the wonder higher;
When to her organ vocal breath was given,
An angel heard, and straight appeared
    Mistaking earth for heaven.

As from the power of sacred lays
    The spheres began to move,
And sung the great Creator's praise
    To all the blessed above;
So when the last and dreadful hour
This crumbling pageant shall devour,
The trumpet shall be heard on high,
The dead shall live, the living die.
And Music shall out tune the sky.

JOHN DRYDEN

⁖DAFFODILS⁖

I wandered lonly as a cloud
   That floats on high o'er vales and hills,
When all at once I saw a crowd—
   A host of golden daffodils
Beside the lake, beneath the trees,
Fluttering and dancing in the breeze.

Continuous as the stars that shine
   And twinkle on the milky way,
They stretched in never-ending line
   Along the margin of the bay:
Ten thousand saw I, at a glance,
Tossing their heads in sprightly dance.

The waves beside them danced, but they
   Outdid the sparkling waves in glee;
A poet could not but be gay,
   In such a jocund company;
I gazed and gazed, but little thought
What wealth the show to me had brought.

For oft, when on my couch I lie,
   In vacant or in pensive mood,
They flash upon that inward eye
   Which is the bliss of solitude,
And when my heart with pleasure fills,
And dances with the daffodills.

              WILLIAM WORDSWORTH.

➤✳HOHENLINDEN✳⬅

On Linden, when the sun was low,
All bloodless lay the untrodden snow,
And dark as winter was the flow
Of Iser rolling rapidly.

But Linden saw another sight
When the drum beat, at dead of night,
Commanding fires of death to light
The darkness of her scenery,

By torch and trumpet fast arrayed,
Each horseman drew his battle blade,
And furious every charger neighed,
To join the dreadful revelry.

Then shook the hills with thunder riven,
Then rushed the steed to battle driven,
And louder than the bolts of heaven
Far flashed the red artillery.

But redder yet that light shall glow
On Linden's hills of stained snow,
And bloodier yet the torrent flow
Of Iser, rolling rapidly.

'T is morn, scarce yon level sun
Can pierce the war-clouds, rolling dun,
Where furious Frank and fiery Hun
Shout in their sulphurous canopy,

The combat deepens. On ye brave,
Who rush to glory, or the grave!
Wave, Munich! all thy banners wave,
And charge with all thy chivalry!

Few, few shall part where many meet!
The snow shall be their winding-sheet,
And every turf beneath their feet
Shall be a soldier's sepulchre.

Thomas Campbell.

∴ BREAK ∴ BREAK ∴ BREAK ∴

Break, break, break.
  On thy cold gray stone, O sea!
And I would that my tongue could utter
  The thoughts that are in me.

O well for the fisherman's boy,
  That he shouts with his sister at play!
O well for the sailor lad
  That he sings in his boat on the bay!

And the stately ships go on,
  To the haven under the hill;
But O for touch of a vanished hand.
  And the sound of a voice that is still!

Break, break, break
  At the foot of thy crags, O sea!
But the tender grace of a day that is dead
  Will never come back to me.

Alfred Tennyson.

❖RECOLLECTIONS❖

YEARS upon years, and the flame of love's high altar
Trembles and sinks, and sense of listening ears
Heeds not the sound it heard of love's blithe psalter
    Years upon years.

Only the sense of a heart that hearkens hears,
Louder than draems that assail and doubts that palter,
Sorrow that sleeps, and that wakes ere sundown peers.

Wakes, that the heart may behold, and yet not falter,
Faces of children as stars unknown of, spheres
Seen but of love, that endure though all things alter,
    Years upon years.

ALGERNON CHARLES SWINBURNE.

❖GATHER·YE✛ROSEBUDS❖

GATHER ye rosebuds while you may,
    Old time is still a-flying;
And this same flower that smiles to-day,
    To-morrow may be dying.

The glorious lamp of heaven, the sun,
    The higher he's a-getting,
The sooner will his race be run
    And nearer he's to setting.

The age is best which is the first,
    When youth and blood are warmer;
But being spent, the worse and worst
    Times still succeed the former.

ROBERT HERRICK.

➤※CHEVY-CHASE※◄

God prosper long our noble king,
  Our lives and safeties all:
A woful hunting once there did
  In Chevy-Chase befall.

To drive the deer with hound and horn
  Earl Percy took his way :
The child may rue that is unborn
  The hunting of that day.

The stout earl of Northumberland
  A vow to God did make,
His pleasure in the Scottish woods
  Three summer days did take—

The chiefest harts in Chevy-Chase
  To kill and bear away.
These tidings to Earl Douglas came,
  In Scotland where he lay ;

He sent Earl Percy present word
  He would prevent his sport.
The English earl, not fearing that,
  Did to the woods resort.

With fifteen hundred bowmen bold,
  All chosen men of might ;
Full well they knew in time of need
  To aim their shafts aright.

On Monday they began to hunt
  As day-light did appear ;
The gallant greyhounds swiftly ran
  Chasing the fallow deer ;

And long before high noon they had
  A hundred fat bucks slain ;
Then having dined, the drovers went
  To rouse the deer again.

The hounds ran swiftly through the woods,
  The nimble deer to take,
That with their cries the hills and dales
  An echo shrill did make;

Lord Percy to the quarry went,
  To view the slaughtered deer ;
Quoth he, "Earl Douglas promised
  This day to meet me here ;

But if I thought he would not come,
  No longer would I stay ;"
With that a brave young gentleman
  Thus to the earl did say :

"Lo, yonder doth Earl Douglas come,
  His men in armor bright ;
Full twenty hundred Scottish spears
  All marching in our sight ;

All men of pleasant Teviotdale,
  Fast by the river Tweed ;"
"Then cease your sports," Earl Percy said,
  And take your bows with speed ;

And now with me, my countrymen,
  Your courage forth advance ;
For never was there champion yet,
  In Scotland or in France,

That ever did on horseback come,
  But if my hap it were,
I durst encounter man for man,
  With him to break a spear."

Earl Douglas on his milk-white steed,
  Most ike a baron bold,
Rode foremost of his company,
  Whose armor shone like gold.

"Show me," said he, "whose men you be"
  That hunt so boldly here,
That, without my consent, do chase
  And kill my fallow-deer."

The first man that did answer make,
  Was noble Percy he—
Who said, "We list not to declare,
  Nor show whose men we be:

"Yet will we spend our dearest blood
  Thy chiefest harts to slay."
Then Douglas swore a solemn oath,
  And thus in rage did say:

"Ere thus I will out-braved be,
  One of us two shall die;
I know thee well, an earl thou art—
  Lord Percy, so am I.

But trust me, Percy, pity it were,
  And great offense. to kill
Any of these our guiltless men,
  For they have done no ill.

Let you and me the battle try,
  And set our men aside "
"Accursed be he," Earl Percy said,
  "By whom this is denied."

Then stepped a gallant squire forth,
  Witherington was his name,
Who said, "I would not have it told
  To Henry, our king, for shame,

"That e'er my captain fought on foot,
  And I stood looking on.
You two be earls," said Witherington,
  "And I a squire alone;

"I'll do the best that do I may,
  While I have power to stand;
While I have power to wield my sword,
  I'll fight with heart and hand."

Our English archers bent their bows—
  Their hearts were good and true;
At the first flight of arrows sent,
  Full fourscore Scots they slew,

Yet stays Earl Douglas on the bent,
  As chieftain stout and good;
As valiant captain, all unmoved,
  The shock he firmly stood.

His host he parted had in three,
  As leader ware and tried;
And soon his spearmen on their foes
  Bore down on every side.

Throughout the English archery
  They dealt full many a wound;
But sill our valiant Englishmen
  All firmly kept their ground.

And throwing straight their bows away,
  They grasped their swords so bright;
And now sharp blows, a heavy shower,
  On shields and helmets light.

They closed full fast on every side—
  No slackness there was found;
And many a gallant gentleman
  Lay gasping on the ground.

At last these two stout earls did meet :
  Like captains of great might,
Like lions wode, they laid on lode,
  And made a cruel fight.

They fought until they both did sweat,
  With swords of tempered steel.
Until the blood, like drops of rain,
  They trickling down did feel.

"Yield thee, Lord Percy,"Doug as said ;
  "In faith I will thee bring
Where thou shalt high advanced be
  By James, our Scottish king.

"Thy ransom I will freely give,
  And this report of thee,
Thou art the most courageous knight
  That ever I did see."

"No, Douglas,"saith Earl Percy then,
  "Thy proffer I do scorn ;
I will not yield to any Scot
  That ever yet was born."

With that there came an arrow keen
  Out of an English bow,
Which struck Earl Douglas to the heart,
  A deep and deadly blow ;

Who never spoke more words than these :
  "Fight on, my merry men all ;
For why, my life is at an end ;
  Lord Percy sees my fall."

Then leaving life, Earl Percy took
  The dead man by the hand ;
And said,"Earl Douglas, for thy life
  Would I had lost my land.

"In truth my very heart doth bleed
 With sorrow for thy sake ;
For sure a more redoubted knight
 Mischance did never take."

A knight amongst the Scots there was
 Who saw Earl Douglas die,
Who straight in wrath did vow revenge
 Upon the Earl Percy.

Sir Hugh Mountgomery was he called,
 Who, with a spear full bright,
Well mounted on a gallant steed,
 Ran fiercely through the fight ;

And past the English archers all,
 Without a dread of fear ;
And through Earl Percy's body then
 He thrust his hateful spear ;

So thus did both these nobles die,
 Whose courage none could stain.
An English archer then perceived
 The noble earl was slain.

Against Sir Hugh Mountgomery
 Then right his shaft he set,
And the gray goose wing that was thereon
 In his heart's blood was wet.

This fight did last from break of day
 Till setting of the sun :
For when they rung the evening-bell,
 The battle scarce was done.

And with Sir George and stout Sir James,
 Both knights of good account,
Good Sir Ralph Raby there was slain,
 Whose prowess did surmount.

For Witherington my heart is wo
  That ever he slain should be,
For when his legs were hewn in two,
  He knelt and fought on his knee.

And with Earl Douglas there was slain
  Sir Hugh Mountgomery,
Sir Charles Murray, that from the field
  One foot would never flee.

Sir Charles Murray of Ratcliff, too—
  His sister's son was he;
Sir David Lamb, so well esteemed,
  But saved he could not be.

And the Lord Maxwell in like case
  Did with Earl Douglas die:
Of twenty hundred Scottish spears,
  Scarce fifty-five did fly.

Of fifteen hundred Englishmen,
  Went home but fifty-three;
The rest in Chevy-Chase were slain,
  Under the greenwood tree.

Next day did many widows come,
  Their husbands to bewail;
They washed their wounds in brinish tears,
  But all would not prevail.

Their bodies, bathed in purple blood,
  They bore with them away:
They kissed the dead a thousand times,
  Ere they were clad in clay.

"Oh heavy news," King James did say;
  "Scotland can witness be
I have not any captain more
  Of such account as he."

Like tidings to King Henry came
  Within as short a space,
That Percy of Northumberland
  Was slain in Chevy-Chase:

"Now God be with him,"said our king,
  "Since 'twill no better be .
I trust I have within my realm
  Five hundred as good as he:

"Yet shall not Scots or Scotland say
  But I will vengeance take:
I'll be revenged on them all,
  For brave Earl Percy's sake."

This vow full well the king performed
  After at Humbledon;
In one day fifty knights were slain,
  With lords of high renown ;

And of the best ,of small account,
  Did many hundreds die:
Thus endeth the hunting of Chevy-Chase,
  Made by Earl Percy.

God save the king, and bless this land,
  With plenty, joy, and peace;
And grant, henceforth, that foul debate
  'Twixt noblemen may cease!
                                    ANONYMOUS.

❖ FLOWERS ❖ WITHOUT ❖ FRUIT ❖

PRUNE thou thy words; the thoughts control
  That o'er thee swell and throng;—
They will condense within thy soul,
  And change to purpose strong.

But he who lets his feelings run
  In soft luxurious flow,
Shrinks when hard service must be done,
  And faints at every woe.

Faith's meanest deed more favour bears,
  Where hearts and wills are weighed,
Than brightest transports, choicest prayers,
  Which bloom their hour, and fade.

JOHN HENRY NEWMAN.

➤ ❖ ST. ❖ MONICA ❖ ←

" AH, could thy grave at home, at Carthage, be !—
  Care not for that, and lay me where I fa'l !
  Everywhere heard will be the judgment call ;
But at God's altar, oh ! remember me."

Thus Monica, and died in Italy.
  Yet fervent had her longing been, through all
  Her course, for home at last, and burial
With her own husband, by the Libyan Sea.

Had been ! but at the end, to her pure soul
All tie with all beside seem'd vain and cheap,
And union before God the only care.

MATTHEW ARNOLD.

⊹ELEGY·WRITTEN·IN·A·COUNTRY⊹ ·:·CHURCHYARD·:·

The curfew tolls the knell of parting day;
  The lowing herd winds slowly o'er the lea;
The ploughman homeward plods his weary way,
  And leaves the world to darkness and to me.

Now fades the glimmering landscape on the sight,
  And all the air a solemn stillness holds,
Save where the beetle wheels his droning flight,
  And drowsy tinklings lull the distant folds;

Save that, from yonder ivy-mantled tower,
  The moping owl does to the moon complain
Of such as, wandering near her secret bower,
  Molest her ancient, solitary reign.

Beneath those rugged elms, that yew-tree's shade,
  Where heaves the turf in many a mouldering heap,
Each in his narrow cell forever laid,
  The rude forefathers of the hamlet sleep.

The breezy call of incense-breathing morn,
  The swallow twittering from the straw-built shed,
The cock's shrill clarion, or the echoing horn,
  No more shall rouse them from their lowly bed.

For them no more the blazing hearth shall burn,
  Or busy housewife ply her evening care
No children run to lisp their sire's return,
  Or climb his knees the envied kiss to share.

4

Oft did the harvest to their sickle yield,
    Their furrow oft the stubborn glebe has broke;
How jocund did they drive their team afield !
    How bowed the woods beneath their sturdy stroke !

Let not ambition mock their useful toil,
    Their homely joys, and destiny obscure;
Nor grandeur hear with a disdainful smile
    The short and simple annals of the poor.

The boast of heraldry, the pomp of power,
    And all that beauty, all that wealth e'er gave,
Await alike the inevitable hour;
    The paths of glory lead but to the grave.

Nor you, ye proud, impute to these the fault,
    If memory o'er their tomb no trophies raise,
Where, through the long-drawn aisle and fretted vault,
    The pealing anthem swells the note of praise.

Can storied urn, or animated bust,
    Back to its mansion call the fleeting breath ?
Can honour's voice provoke the silent dust,
    Or flattery soothe the dull, cold ear of death ?

Perhaps in this neglected spot is laid
    Some heart once pregnant with celestial fire;
Hands that the rod of empire might have swayed,
    Or waked to ecstasy the living lyre;

But knowledge to their eyes her ample page,
    Rich with the spoils of time, did ne'er unrol;
Chill penury repressed their noble rage,
    And froze the genial current of the soul.

Full many a gem of purest ray serene
    The dark, unfathomed caves of ocean bear;
Full many a flower is born to blush unseen,
    And waste its sweetness on the desert air.

Some village Hampden, that, wih dauntless breast,
  The little tyrant of his fields withstood ;
Some mute, inglorious Milton here may rest ;
  Some Cromwell, guiltless of his country's blood.

The applause of listening senates to command,
  The threats of pain and ruin to despise,
To scatter plenty o'er a smiling land,
  And read their history in a nation's eyes,

Their lot forbade : nor circumscribed alone
  Their growing virtues, but their crimes confined ;
Forbade to wade through slaughter to a throne,
  And shut the gates of mercy to mankind ;

The struggling pangs of conscious truth to hide,
  To quench the blushes of ingenious shame,
Or heap the shrine of luxury and pride
  With incense kindled at the muse's flame.

Far from the madding crowd's ignoble strife,
  Their sober wishes never learned to stray ;
Along the cool, seque-tered vale of life
  They kept the noisless tenour of their way.

Yet even these bones from insult to protect,
  Some frail memorial still erected nigh,
With uncouth rhymes and shapeless sculpture decked,
  Implores the passing tribute of a sigh.

Their name, their years, spelt by the unletterd muse,
  The place of fame and elegy supply ;
And many a holy text around she strews,
  That teach the rustic moralist to die.

For who, to dumb forgetfulness a prey,
  This pleasing, anxious being e'er resigned,
Left the warm precincts of the chreeful day,
  Nor cast one longing, lingering look behind ?

On some fond breast the parting soul relies,
   Some pious drops the closing eye requires;
E'en from the tomb the voice of Nature cries,
   E'en in our ashes live their wonted fires.

For thee, who, mindful of the unhonoured dead,
   Dost in these lines their artless tales relate;
If chance, by lonely contemplation led,
   Some kindred spirit shall enquire thy fate,

Haply some hoary-headed swain may say:—
   "Oft have I seen him, at the peep of dawn,
Brushing with hasty steps the dews away,
   To meet the sun upon the upland lawn.

"There at the foot of yonder nodding beech,
   That wreathes its old, fantastic roots so high
His listless length at noontide would he stretch,
   And pore upon the brook that babbles by.

"Hard by yon wood, now smiling as in scorn,
   Muttering his wayward fancies, he would rove;
Now drooping, woful-wan, like one forlorn,
   Or crazed with care, or crossed in hopeless love.

"One morn I missed him on the customed hill,
   Along the heath, and near his favourite tree;
Another came,—nor yet beside the rill;
   Nor up the lawn, nor at the wood was he;

"The next, with dirges due, in sad array,
   Slow through the church-way path we saw him borne;
Approach and read (for thou canst read) the lay,
   Graved on the stone beneath yon aged thorn."

THE EPITAPH.

Here rests his head upon the lap of earth,
  A youth to fortune and to fame unknown;
Fair science frowned not on his humble birth,
  And melancholy marked him for her own.

Large was his bounty, and his soul sincere;
  Heaven did a recompense as largely send;
He gave to misery, (all he had), a tear,
  He gained from heaven('t was all he wished) a friend.

No further seek his merits to disclose,
  Or draw his frailites from their dread abode,—
(There they alike in trembling hope repose,)
  The bosom of his Father and his God.

THOMAS GRAY.

✠CHILDHOOD✠

In my poor mind it is most sweet to muse
Upon the days gone by; to act in thought
Past seasons o'er, and be again a child;
To sit in fancy on the turf-clad slope,
Down which the child would roll; to pluck gay flowers,

Make posies in the sun, which the child's hand
(Childhood offended soon, soon reconciled),
Would throw away, and straight take up again,
Then fling them to the winds, and o'er the lawn
Bound with so playful and so light a foot,
That the pressed daisy scarce declined her head.

CHARLES LAMB.

→✦WE·ARE·SEVEN✦←

A SIMPLE child,
That lightly draws its breath,
And feels its life in every limb,
What should it know of death?

I met a little cottage girl:
She was eight years old, she said;
Her hair was thick with many a curl
That clustered round her head.

She had a rustic, woodland air,
And she was wildly clad;
Her eyes were fair, and very fair;—
Her beauty made me glad.

"Sisters and brothers, little maid,
How many may you be?"
"How many? Seven in all," she said,
And wondering looked at me.

"And where are they? I pray you tell."
She answered, "Seven are we;
And two of us at Conway dwell,
And two are gone to sea;

"Two of us in the churchyard lie,
My sister and my brother;
And, in the churchyard cottage, I
Dwell near them with my mother."

"You say that two at Conway dwell,
And two are gone to sea,
Yet ye are seven! I pray you tell,
Sweet maid, how this may be."

Then did the little maid reply,
  "Seven boys and girls are we;
Two of us in the churchyard lie
  Beneath the churchyard tree."

"You run about, my little maid;
  Your limbs they are alive;
If two are in the churchyard laid,
  Then ye are only five."

"Their graves are green, they may be seen,"
  The little maid replied;
"Twelve steps or more from my mother's door,
  And they are side by side.

"My stockings there I often knit,
  My kerchief there I hem;
And there upon the ground I sit,
  And sing a song to them.

"And often after sun-set, sir,
  When it is light and fair,
I take my little porringer,
  And eat my supper there.

"The first that died was Sister Jane;
  In bed she moaning lay,
Till God released her of her pain;
  And then she went away.

"So in the churchyard she was laid;
  And, when the grass was dry,
Together round her grave we played,
  My brother John and I.

"And when the ground was white with snow,
  And I could run and slide,
My brother John was forced to go,
  And he lies by her side."

"How many are you, then," said I,
  "If they are two in heaven?"
Quick was the little maid's reply!
  "O Master, we are seven."

"But they are dead; those two are dead!
  Their spirits are in heaven!
'T was throwing words away; for still
The little maid would have her will,
  And said, "Nay, we are seven."
                              WILLIAM WORDSWORTH.

GOD'S ACRE.

I LIKE that ancient Saxon phrase which calls
  The burial-ground God's-Acre! It is just;
It consecrates each grave within its walls,
  And breathes a benison o'er the sceping dust.

God's-Acre! Yes, that blessed name imparts
  Comfort to those who in the grave have sown
The seed that they had garnered in their hearts,
  Their bread of life, alas! no more their own.

Into its furrows shall we all be cast,
  In the sure faith that we shall rise again
At the great harvest, when the archangel's blast
  Shall winnow, like a fan, the chaff and grain.

Then shall the good stand in immortal bloom,
  In the fair gardens of that second birth;
And each bright blossom mingle its perfume
  With that of flowers which never bloomed on earth.

With thy rude ploughshare, Death, turn up the sod,
  And spread the furrow for the seed we sow;
This is the field and Acre of our God,
  This is the place where human harvests grow!
                              HENRY WADSWORTH LONGFELLOW.

❖THANATOPSIS❖

To him who in the 'ove of nature holds
Communion with her visible forms, she speaks
A various language; for his gayer hours
She has a voice of gladness, and a smile
And eloquence of beauty; and she glides
Into his darker musings with a mild
And healing sympathy, that steals away
Their sharpness ere he is aware.   When thoughts
Of the last bitter hour comes like a blight
Over thy spirit, and sad images
Of the stern agony, and shroud, and pall,
And breathless darkness, and the narrow house,
Make thee to shudder, and grow sick at heart—
Go forth, under the open sky, and list
To nature's teachings, while from all around—
Earth and her waters, and the depth of air—
Comes a still voice : Yet a few days, and thee
The all-beholding sun shall see no more
In all his course; nor yet in the cold ground,
Where thy pale form was laid with many tears,
Nor in the embrace of ocean shall exist
Thy image. Earth, that nourished thee, shall claim
Thy growth to be resolved to earth again;
And, lost each human trace, surrendering up
Thine individual being, shalt thou go
To mix for ever with the elements—
To be a brother to the insensible rock,
And to the sluggish clod which the rude swain
Turns with his share, and treads upon.   The oak
Shall send his roots abroad, and pierce thy mould.
Yet not to thine eternal resting-place
Shalt thou retire alone, nor couldst thou wish

Couch more magnificent. Thou shalt lie down
With patriarchs of the infant world—with kings,
The powerful of the earth—the wise, the good—
Fair forms, and hoary seers of ages past,
All in one mighty sepulchre. The hills
Rock-ribbed and ancient as the sun,—the vales
Stretching in pensive quietness between—
The venerable woods—rivers that move
In majesty, and the complaining brooks
That make the meadows green; and, poured round all,
Old ocean's gray and melancholy waste,—
Are but the solemn decorations all
Of the great tomb of man. The golden sun,
The planets, all the infinite host of heaven,
Are shining on the sad abodes of death,
Through the still lapse of ages. All that tread
The globe are but a handful to the tribes
That slumber in its bosom.—Take the wings
Of morning: traverse Barca's desert sands,
Or lose thyself in the continuous woods
Where rolls the Oregon, and hears no sound
Save his own dashings—yet, the dead are there;
And millions in the solitudes, since first
The flight of years began, have laid them down
In their last sleep—the dead reign there alone.
So shalt thou rest; and what if thou withdraw
In silence from the living, and no friend
Take note of thy departure? All that breathe
Will share thy destiny. The gay will laugh
When thou art gone, the solemn brood of care
Plod on, and each one as before will chase
His favourite phantom; yet all these shall leave
Their mirth and their employments, and shall come
And make their bed with thee. As the long train
Of ages glides away, the sons of men,
The youth in life's green spring, and he who goes
In the full strength of years—matron, and maid,

And the sweet babe, and the gray-headed man,—
Shall one by one be gathered to thy side
By those who in their turn shall follow them.
So live, that when thy summons comes to join
The innumerable caravan which moves
To that mysterious realm where each shall take
His chamber in the silent halls of death,
Thou go not like the quarry-slave at night,
Scourged to his dungeon; but, sustained and soothed
By an unfaltering trust, approach thy grave
Like one who wraps the drapery of his couch
About him, and lies down to pleasant dreams.

WILLIAM CULLEN BRYANT.

➤❖SONNET❖◄

THE world is too much with us; late and soon,
  Getting and spending, we lay waste our powers;
  Little we see in nature that is ours;
We have given our hearts away, a sordid boon!
This sea that bares her bosom to the moon;
  The Winds that will be howling at all hours,
  And are up-gathered now like sleeping flowers;
For this, for every thing, we are out of tune:
It moves us not.—Great God! I'd rather be
  A pagan suckled in a creed outworn;
So might I, standing on this pleasant lea,
  Have glimpses that would make me less forlorn;
Have sight of Proteus rising from the sea,
  Or hear old Triton blow his wreathéd horn.

WILLIAM WORDSWORTH.

→✲VEXILLA✚REGIS✲←

The royal banners forward go,
The cr ss shines forth in mystic glow,
Where He in flesh, our flesh who made,
Our sentence bore, our ransom paid :

Where deep for us the spear was dyed,
Life's torrent rushing from His side,
To wash us in that precious flood
Where mingled water flowed and blood.

Fulfilled is all that David told
In true prophetic song of old :
Amidst the nations, God, saith he,
Hath reigned and triumphed from a tree.

O tree of beauty, tree of light!
O tree with royal purple dight!
Elect on whose triumphal breast
Those holy limbs should find their rest!

On whose dear arms, so widely flung,
The weight of the world's ransom hung—
The price of human kind to pay,
And spoil the spoiler of his prey.

To Thee, eternal three in one,
Let homage meet by all be done,
Whom by the cross Thou dost restore,
Preserve and govern evermore.   Amen.

VENANTIUS FORTUNATUS.

Anonymous Translation.

✢FOLDING·THE·FLOCKS✢

SHEPHERDS all, and maidens fair,
Fold your flocks up; for the air
'Gins to thicken, and the sun
Already his great course hath run.
See the dew-drops, how they kiss
Every little flower that is:
Hanging on their velvet heads,
Like a string of crystal beads.
See the heavy clouds low falling
And bright Hesperus down calling
The dead night from under ground;
At whose rising, mists unsound,
Damps and vapours, fly apace,
And hover o'er the smiling face
Of these pastures; where they come,
Striking dead both bud and bloom.
Therefore from such danger lock
Every one his loved flock;
And let your dogs lie loose without,
Lest the wolf come like a scout
From the mountain, and, ere day,
Bear a lamb or kid away;
Or the crafty, thievish fox,
Break upon your simple flocks.
To rescue yourself from these,
Be not too secure in ease;
So shall you good shepherds prove,
And deserve your master's love.
Now, good night! may sweetest slumbers
And soft silence fall in numbers
On your eyelids. So farewell:
Thus I end my evening knell.

BEAUMONT AND FLETCHER.

REBECCA'S HYMN

FROM "IVANHOE."

WHEN Israel, of the Lord beloved,
  Out from the land of bondage came,
Her father's God before her moved,
  An awful guide in smoke and flame.
By day, along the astonished lands
  The cloudy pillar glided slow ;
By night, Arabia's crimsoned sands
  Returned the fiery column's glow.

There rose the choral hymn of praise,
  And trump and timbrel answered keen ;
And Zion's daughters poured their lays,
  With priest's and warrior's voice between.
No potents now our foes amaze—
  Forsaken Israel wanders lone ;
Our fathers would not know Thy ways,
  And thou hast left them to their own.

But, present still, though now unseen,
  When brightly shines the prosperous day,
Be thoughts of Thee a cloudy screen,
  To temper the deceitful ray.
And O, when stoops on Judah's path
  In shade and storm the frequent night,
Be thou, long-suffering, slow to wrath,
  A burning and a shining light!

Our harps we left by Babel's streams—
  The tyrant's jest, the Gentile's scorn ;
No censer round our altar beams,
  And mute are timbrel, trump, and horn.
But thou hast said, the blood of goats,
  The flesh of rams, I will not prize—
A contrite heart, and humble thoughts,
  Are mine accepted sacrifice.

SIR WALTER SCOTT.

->GRASSHOPPER·AND·CRICKET<-

GREEN little vaulter in the sunny grass,
Catching your heart up at the field of June—
Sole voice that's heard amidst the lazy noon
When even the bees lag at the summoning brass ;
And you, warm little housekeeper, who class
With those who think the candles come too soon,
Loving the fire, and with your tricksome tune
Nick the glad silent moments as they pass !
O sweet and tiny cousins, that belong ,
One the fields, the other to the hearth,
Both have your sunshine : both, though small, are strong
At your clear hearts ; and both seem given to earth
To sing in thoughtful ears this natural song—
In doors and out, summer and winter, mirth.
LEIGH HUNT.

->GRASSHOPPER·AND·CRICKET<-

THE poetry of earth is never dead :
When all the birds are faint with the hot sun
And hide in cooling trees, a voice will run
From hedge to hedge about the new-mown mead.
That is the Grasshopper's—he takes the lead
In summer luxury,—he has never done
With his delights ; for, when tired out with fun,
He rests at ease beneath some pleasant weed.
The poetry of earth is ceasing never.
On a lone winter evening, when the frost
Has wrought a silence, from the stove there shrills
The Cricket's song, in warmth increasing ever,
And seems, to one in drowsiness half lost,
The Grasshopper's among some grassy hills.
JOHN KEATS.

➤✳TO✦THE✦SKYLARK✳⬅

HAIL to thee, blithe spirit!
　Bird thou never wert,
That from heaven, or near it,
　Pourest thy full heart
In profuse strains of unpremeditated art.

Higher still and higher
　From the earth thou springest,
Like a cloud of fire;
　The blue deep thou wingest,
And singing still dost soar, and soaring ever singest.

In the golden lightning
　Of the setting sun,
O'er which clouds are brightening,
　Thou dost float and run;
Like an embodied joy whose race is just begun.

The pale, purple even
　Melts around thy flight;
Like a star of heaven,
　In the broad daylight,
Thou art unseen, but yet I hear thy shrill delight.

Keen as are the arrows
　Of that silver sphere,
Whose intense lamp narrows
　In the white dawn clear,
Until we hardly see, we feel that it is there.

All the earth and air
　With thy voice is loud,
As, when night is bare,
　From one lonely cloud
The moon rains out her beams, and heaven is overflowed.

What thou art we know not;
  What is most like thee?
From rainbow-clouds there flow not
  Drops so bright to see,
As from thy presence showers a rain of melody.

Like a poet hidden
  In the light of thought,
Singing hymns unbidden,
  Till the world is wrought
To sympathy with hopes and fears it heeded not;

Like a high-born maiden,
  In a palace tower,
Soothing her love-laden
  Soul in secret hour
With music sweet as love, which overflows her bower;

Like a glow-worm go'den,
  In a dell of dew,
Scattering unbeholden
  Its aerial hue
Among the flowers and grass which screen it from the
  view;

Like a rose embowered
  In its own green leaves,
By warm winds deflowered,
  Till the scent it gives
Makes faint with too much sweet these heavy-winged
  thieves.

Sound of vernal showers
  On the twinkling grass,
Rain-awakened flowers,
  All that ever was
Joyous, and fresh, and clear, thy music doth surpass.

6

Teach us, sprite or bird,
   What sweet thoughts are thine:
I have never heard
   Praise of love or wine
That panted forth a flood of rapture so divine.

   Chorus hymeneal,
     Or triumphant chant,
   Matched with thine would be all
     But an empty vaunt—
A thing wherein we feel there is some hidden want.

   What objects are the fountains
     Of thy happy strain ?
   What fields, or waves, or mountains?
     What shapes of sky or plain ?
What love of thine own kind? what ignorance of pain ?

   With thy clear, keen joy and
     Langour cannot be ;
   Shadow of annoyance
     Never came near thee ;
Thou lovest, but ne'er knew love's sad satiety.

   Waking or asleep,
     Thou of death must deem
   Things more true and deep
     Than we mortals dream ;
Or how could thy notes flow in such a crystal stream ?

   We look before and after,
     And pine for what is not:
   Our sincerest laughter
     With some pain is fraught;
Our sweetest songs are those that tell of saddest thought.

   Yet if we could scorn
     Hate, and pride, and fear;
   If we were things born
     Not to shed a tear,
I know not how thy joy we ever should come near.

Better than all measures
Of delightful sound;
Better than all treasures
That in books are found,
Thy skill to poet were, thou scorner of the ground.

Teach me half the gladness
That thy brain must know,
Such harmonious madness
From my lips would flow,
The world should listen then, as I am listening now.
PERCY BYSSHE SHELLEY.

⁙LOST·DAYS⁙

The lost days of my life until to day,
What were they, could I see them on the street
Lie as they fell?　Would they be ears of wheat
Sown once for food but trodden into clay?
Or golden coins squandered and still to pay?
Or drops of blood dabbling the guilty feet?
Or such spilt water as in dreams must cheat
The throats of men in hell, who thirst alway?

I do not see them here: but after death
God knows I know the faces I shall see,
Each one a murdered self, with low last breath.
I am thyself,—what hast thou done to me?
And I—and I—thyself: (lo! each one saith,)
And thou thyself to all eternity!
DANTE GABRIEL ROSSETTI.

➤✦AVE✦◄

Mother of the Fair Delight,
Thou handmaid perfect in God's sight,
Now sitting fourth beside the Three,
Thyself a women-Trinity,—
Being a daughter born to God,
Mother of Christ from stall to rood,
And spouse unto the Holy Ghost :—
Oh when our need is uttermost,
Think that to such as death may strike
Thou once wert sister sisterlike !
Thou headstone of humanity,
Groundstone of the great Mystery,
Fashioned like us, yet more than we !

Mind'st thou not (when June's heavy breath
Warmed the long days in Nazareth,)
That eve thou didst go forth to give
Thy flowers some drink that they might live
One faint night more amid the sands?
Far off the trees were as pale wands
Aga'nst the fervid sky : the sea
Sighed further off eternally
As human sorrow sighs in sleep.
Then suddenly the awe grew deep,
As of a day to which all days
Were footsteps in God's secret ways :
Until a folding sense, like prayer,
Which is, as God is, everywhere,
Gathered about thee ; and a voice
Spoke to thee without any noise,
Being of the silence :— "Hail," it said,
"Thou that art highly favored ;
The Lord is with thee here and now ;
Blessed among all women thou."

Ah! knew'st thou of the end, when first
'That Babe was on thy bosom nursed?—
Or when He tottered round thy thy knee
Did thy great sorrow dawn on thee?—
And through His boyhood, year by year
Eating with Him the passover
Didst thou discern confusedly
That holier sacrament, when He,
The bitter cup about to quaff,
Should break the bread and eat thereof?—
Or came not yet the knowledge, even
'Till on some day forecast in heaven
His feet passed through thy door to press
Upon His Father's business?
Or still was God's high secret kept?

Nay, but I think the whisper crept
Like growth through childhood.   Work and play,
Things common to the course of day,
Awed thee with meanings unfulfill'd;
And all through girlhood, something still'd
Thy senses, like the birth of light,
When thou hast trimmed thy lamp at night
Or washed thy garments in the stream;
To whose white bed had come the dream
That He was thine and thou wast His
Who feeds among the field-lilies.
O solemn shadow of the end
In that wise spirit long contained!
O awful end! and those unsaid
Long years when It was Finishéd!

Mind'st thou not; (when the twilight gone
Left darkness in the house of John,)
Between the naked window-bars
That spacious vigil of the stars!—
For thou, a watcher even as they,
Wouldst rise from where throughout the day

Thou wroughtest raiment for His poor;
And, finding the fixed terms endure
Of day and night which never brought
Sounds of His coming chariot,
Wouldst lift through cloud-waste unexplor'd
Those eyes that said, "How long, O Lord?"
Then that diciple whom He loved
Well heeding, haply would be moved
To ask thy blessing in His name;
And that one thought in both, the same
Though silent, then would clasp ye round
To weep together,—tears long bound,
Sick tears of patience, dumb and slow.
Yet, "Surely I come quickly,"—so
He said, from life and death gone home.
Amen : even so, Lord Jesus, come!

But oh! what human tongue can speak
That day when death was sent to break
From the tir'd spirit, like a veil,
Its covenant with Gabriel
Endured at length unto the end?
What human thought can apprehend
That mystery of motherhood
When thy Beloved at length renewed
The sweet communion severed,—
His left hand underneath thy head
And His right hand embracing thee?—
Lo! He was thine, and this is He!

Soul, is it Faith, or Love, or Hope,
That lets me see her standing
Where the light of the Throne is bright?
Unto the left, unto the right,
The cherubim, arrayed, conjoint,
Float inward to a golden point,
And from between the seraphim
The glory issues for a hymn.

O Mary Mother, be not loth
To listen,—thou whom the stars clothe,
Who seest and mayst not be seen?
Hear us at last, O Mary Queen?
Into our shadow bend thy face,
Bowing thee from thy secret place,
O Mary Virgin, full of grace?

DANTE GABRIEL ROSSETTI.

❖ WAKE AGAIN ! ❖

WAKE again, Teutonic father-ages,
  Speak again, beloved primeval creeds;
Flash ancestral spirit from your pages,
  Wake the greedy age to noble deeds.

Tell us how, of old, our saintly mothers
  Schooled themselves by vigil, fast, and prayer;
Learned to love as Jesus loved before them,
  While they bore the cross which poor men bear.

Tell us how our stout crusading fathers
  Fought and died for God, and not for gold:
Let their love, their faith, their boyish daring,
  Distance-mellowed, gild the days of old.

Tell us how the ceaseless workers, thronging,
  Angel-tended, round the convent-doors,
Wrought to Christian Faith and holy order
  Savage hearts alike and barren moors

Ye who built the churches where we worship,
  Ye who framed the laws by which we move
Fathers, long belied and long forsaken,
  Oh, forgive the children of your love!

CHARLES KINGSLEY.

❖QUA❖CURSUM❖VENTUS❖

As ships, becalmed at eve, that lay
  With canvas drooping, side by side,
Two towers of sail at dawn of day
  Are scarce long leagues apart descried.

When fell the night, up sprang the breeze,
  And all the darkling hours they plied,
Nor dreamed but each the selfsame seas
  By each was cleaving, side by side:

E'en so,—but why the ta'e reveal
  Of those whom, year by year unchanged,
Brief absence joined anew to feel,
  Astounded, soul from soul estranged?

At dead of night their sails were filled,
  And onward each rejoicing steered;—
Ah! neither blame, for neither willed
  Or wist what first with dawn appeared.

To veer, how vain!   On, onward strain,
  Brave barks!   In light, in darkness too,
Through winds and tides one compass guides:
  To that and your own selves be true.

But O blithe breeze! and O great seas!
  Though ne'er, that earliest parting past,
On your wide plain they join again,—
  Together lead them home at last.

One port, methought, alike they sought,—
  One purpose hold where'er they fare;
O bounding breeze, O rushing seas,
  At last, at last, unite them there!

                        ARTHUR HUGH CLOUGH.

❖ THE DESTRUCTION OF SENNACHERIB ❖

The Assyrian came down like a wolf on the fold,
And his cohorts were gleaming in purple and gold;
And the sheen of their spears was like stars on the sea,
When the blue waves roll nightly on deep Galilee.

Like the leaves of the forest when summer is green,
That host with their banners at sunset were seen:
Like the leaves of the forest when autumn hath blown,
That host on the morrow lay withered and strown.

For the Angel of Death spread his wings on the blast,
And breathed in the face of the foe as he passed;
And the eyes of the sleepers waxed deadly and chill,
And their hearts but once heaved, and for ever grew still!

And there lay the steed with his nostril all wide,
But through it there rolled not the breath of his pride:
And the foam of his gasping lay white on the turf,
And cold as the spray of the rock-beating surf.

And there lay the rider distorted and pale,
With the dew on his brow, and the rust on his mail;
And the tents were all silent, the banners alone,
The lances unlifted, the trumpet unblown.

And the widows of Ashur are loud in their wail,
And the idols are broke in the temple of Baal;
And the might of the Gentile, unsmote by the sword,
Hath melted like snow in the glance of the Lord!

GEORGE GORDON BYRON.

→❖BEFORE✢SEDAN❖←

HERE in this leafy place,
  Quiet he lies,
Cold, with his sightless face
  Turned to the skies ;
'T is but another dead ;—
All you can say is said.

Carry his body hence,—
  Kings must have slaves ;
Kings climb to eminence
  Over men's graves.
So this man's eye is dim ;—
Throw the earth over him

What was the white you touched,
  There at his side?
Paper his hand had clutched
  Tight ere he died ;
Message or wish, may be:—
Smooth out the folds and see.

Hardly the worst of us
  Here could have smiled ?—
Only the tremulous
  Words of a child : —
Prattle, that had for stops
Just a few ruddy drops.

Look. She is sad to miss,
  Morning and night,
His—her dead father's —kiss,
  Tries to be bright,
Good to mamma, and sweet.
That is all. *"Marguerite."*

Ah, if beside the dead
   Slumbered the pain?
Ah, if the hearts that bled
   Slept with the slain!
If the grief died!—But no:—
   Death will not have it so.

AUSTIN DOBSON.

❖ TO ✦ THOMAS ✦ MOORE ❖

My boat is on the shore,
   And my bark is on the sea;
But before I go, Tom Moore,
   Here's a double health to thee!

Here's a sigh to those who love me,
   And a smile to those who hate;
And, whatever sky's above me,
   Here's a heart for every fate!

Though the ocean roar around me,
   Yet it still shall bear me on;
Though a desert should surround me,
   It hath springs that may be won.

Were't the last drop in the well,
   As I gasped upon the brink,
Ere my fainting spirit fell,
   'T is to thee that I would drink.

With that water, as this wine,
   The libation I would pour
Should be,—Peace with thine and mine,
   And a health to thee, Tom Moore!

GEORGE GORDON BYRON.

THE WOODSPURGE

The wind flapped loose, the wind was still,
Shaken out dead from tree and hill:
I had walked on at the wind's will,—
I sat now, for the wind was still.

Between my knees my forehead was,—
My lips, drawn in, said not Alas!
My hair was over in the grass,
My naked ears heard the day pass.

My eyes, wide open, had the run
Of some ten weeds to fix upon;
Among those few, out of the sun,
The woodspurge flowered, three cups in one.

From perfect grief there need not be
Wisdom or even memory:
One thing then learnt remains to me,—
The woodspurge has a cup of three.

DANTE GABRIEL ROSSETTI.

LIGHT

THE night has a thousand eyes,
    The day but one;
Yet the light of the bright world dies
    With the dying sun.

The mind has a thousand eyes,
    And the heart but one;
Yet the light of a whole life dies
    When its love is done.

FRANCIS W. BOURDILLON.

❖THE✛DESERTED✛VILLAGE❖

SWEET Auburn! loveliest village of the plain,
Where health and plenty cheered the labouring swain,
Where smiling spring its earliest visit paid,
And parting summer's lingering b ooms delayed.
Dear lovely bowers of innocence and ease,
Seats of my youth when every sport could please'
How often have I loitered o'er thy green,
Where humble happiness endeared each scene!
How often have I paused on every charm,
The sheltered cot, the cultivated farm,
The never failing brook, the busy mill,
The decent church that topped the neighouring hill,
The hawthorn-bush, with seats beneath the shade,
For talking age and whispering lovers made!
How often have I blessed the coming day,
When toil remitting lent its turn to play,
And all the village train, from labour free,
Led up their sports beneath the spreading tree,
While many a pastime circled in the shade,
The young contending as the ol l surveyed ;
And many a gambol frolicked o'er the ground,
And s eights of art and feats of strength went round ;
And still, as each repeated pleasure tired,
Succeeding sports the mirthful band inspired ;
The dancing pair that simply sought renown,
By holding out, to tire each other down ;
The swain mistrustless of his smutted face,
While secret laughter tittered round the place ;
The bashful virgin's sidelong looks of love,
The matron's glance that would these look reprove,—
These were thy charms, sweet village ! sports like these,
With sweet succession, taught e'en toil to please ;

These round thy bowers their cheerful influence shed,
These were thy charms,—but all these charms are fled!
　　Sweet smiling village, 'oveliest of the lawn.
Thy sports are fled, and all thy charms withdrawn:
Amidst thy bowers the tyrant's hand is seen,
And deso ation saddens all thy green;
One only master grasps the whole domain,
And half a tillage stints thy smiling plain;
No more thy glassy brook reflects the day,
But, choked the sedges, works its weary way;
Along thy glades, a solitary guest,
The hollow sounding bittern guards its nest;
Amidst thy desert walks the lapwing flies,
And tires their echoes with unvaried cries.
Sunk are thy bowers in shapeless ruin all,
And the long grass o'ertops the mouldering wall,
And, trembling, shrinking from the spoiler's hand,
Far, far away thy children leave the land.

　　Ill fares the land, to hastening ills a prey,
Where wealth accumulates and men decay:
Princes and lords may flourish, or may fade;
A breath can make them; as a breath has made;
But a bold peasantry, their country's pride,
When once destroyed, can never be supplied.

　　A time there was, ere England's grief began,
When every rood of ground maintained its man;
For him light Labour spread her wholesome store,
Just gave what life required, but gave no more;
His best companions, innocence and health;
And his best riches, ignorance of wealth.

　　But times are altered; trade's unfeeling train
Usurp the land and dispossess the swain;
Along the lawn, where scattered hamlets rose,
Unwieldy wealth and cumbrous pomp repose,
And every want to luxury allied,

And every pang that folly pays to pride.
Those gentle hours that plenty bade to bloom,
Those calm desires that asked but little room,
Those healthful sports that graced the peaceful scene,
Lived in each look, and brightened all the green,—
These far departing, seek a kinder shore,
And rural mirth and manners are no more.

Sweet Auburn! parent of the blissful hour,
Thy glades forlorn confess the tyrant's power.
Here, as I take my solitary rounds,
Amidst thy tangling walks and ruined grounds,
And, many a year elapsed, return to view
Where once the cottage stood, the hawthorn grew,
Rememberance wakes, with all her busy train,
Swells at my breast, and turns the past to pain.

In all my wanderings round this world of care,
In all my griefs—and God has given my share—
I still had hopes my latest hours to crown,
Amidst these humble bowers to lay me down;
To husband out life's taper at the close,
And keep the flame from wasting by repose:
I still had hopes—for pride attends us still—
Amidst the swains to show my book-learned skill,
Around my fire an evening group to draw,
And tell of all I felt and all I saw;
And, as a hare, whom hounds and horns pursue,
Pants to the place from whence at first she flew,
I still had hopes, my long vexation past,
Here to return,—and die at home at last.

O blest retirement! friend to life's decline,
Retreats from care, that never must be mine,
How blest is he who crowns in shades like these.
A youth of labour with an age of ease;
Who quits a world where strong temptations try,
And, since 't is hard to combat, learns to fly!

For him no wretches, born to work and weep,
Explore the mine, or tempt the dangerous deep;
No surly porter stands in guilty state,
To spurn imploring famine from the gate,
But on he moves to meet his later end,
Angels around befriending virtue's friend;
Sinks to the grave with unperceived decay,
While resignation gently slopes the way;
And, all his prospects brightening to the last,
His heaven commences ere the world be past.

   Sweet was the sound, when oft, at evening's close,
Up yonder hill the village murmur rose;
There, as I passed with careless steps and slow,
The mingling notes came softened from below;
The swain responsive as the milkmaid sung,
The sober herd that lowed to meet their young;
The noisy geese that gabbled o'er the pool,
The playful children just let loose from school;
The watch-dog's voice that bayed the whispering wind,
And the loud laugh that spoke the vacant mind,—
These all in sweet confusion sought the shade,
And filled each pause the nightingale had made,
But now the sounds of population fail;
No cheerful murmurs fluctuate in the gale,
No busy steps the grass-grown foot-way tread,
But all the bloomy flush of life is fled.
All but yon widowed, solitary thing,
That feebly bends beside the plashy spring;
She wretched matron, forced in age, for bread,
To strip the brook with mantling cresses spread,
To pick her wintry fagot from the thorn,
To seek her nightly shed, and weep till morn;
She only left of all the harmless train,
The sad historian of the pensive plain.

   Near yonder copse, where once the garden smiled,
And still where many a garden-flower grows wild,

There, where a few torn shrubs the place disclose,
The village preacher's modest mansion rose.
A man he was to all the country dear,
And passing rich with forty pounds a year;
Remote from towns he ran his godly race,
Nor e'er had changed, nor wished to change, his place;
Unskilful he to fawn, or seek for power,
By doctrines fashioned to the varying hour;
Far other aims his heart had learned to prize,
More bent to raise the wretched than to rise
His house was known to all the vagrant train.
He chid their wanderings, but relieved their pain;
The long-remembered beggar was his guest,
Whose beard descending swept his aged breast.
The ruined spendthrift, now no longer proud,
Claimed kindred there, and had his claims allowed;
The broken soldier, kindly bade to stay,
Sate by his fire, and talked the night away;
Wept o'er his wounds, or tales of sorrow done,
Shouldered his crutch, and showed how fields were won.
Pleased with his guests, the good man learned to glow,
And quite forgot their vices in their woe;
Careless their merits or their faults to scan,
His pity gave ere charity began.

Thus to relieve the wretched was his pride,
And e'en his failings leaned to Virtue's side;
But in his duty prompt at every call,
He watched and wept, he prayed and felt for all!
And, as a bird each fond endearment tries,
To tempt its new-fledged offspring to the skies,
He tried each art, reproved each dull delay,
Allured to brighter worlds, and led the way.
Beside the bed where parting life was laid'
And sorrow, guilt, and pain by turns dimayed,
The reverend champion stood. At his control,
Despair and anguish fled the struggling soul;

Comfort came down the trembling wretch to raise,
And his last faltering accents whispered praise.

At church, with meek and unaffected grace,
His looks adorned the venerable place;
Truth from his lips prevailed with double sway,
And fools, who came to scoff, remained to pray.
The service past, around this pious man,
With steady zeal, each honest rustic ran;
E'en children followed with endearing wile,
And plucked his gown, to share the good man's smile
His ready smile a parent's warmth expressed,
Their welfare pleased him, and their cares distressed;
To them his heart, his love, his griefs were given,
But all his serious thoughts had rest in heaven.
As some tall cliff, that lifts its awful form,
Swells from the vale, and midway leaves the storm,
Though round its breast the rolling clouds are spread,
Eternal sunshine settles on its head.

Beside yon straggling fence that skirts the way,
With blossomed furze unprofitably gay,
There in his noisy mansion, skilled to rule.
The village master taught his little school
A man severe he was, and stern to view,
I knew him well, and every truant knew;
Well had the boding tremblers learned to trace
The day's disasters in his morning face;
Full well they laughed with counterfeited glee
At all his jokes, for many a joke had he;
Full well the busy whisper circling round
Conveyed the dismal tidings when he frowned;
Yet he was kind, or, if severe in aught,
The love he bore to learning was in fault.
The village all declared how much he knew,
'T was certain he could write, and cipher too;
Lands he could measure, times and tides presage,
And e'en the story ran that he could gauge;

In arguing too, the parson owned his skill,
For, e'en though vanquished, he could argue still,
While words of learned length and thundering sound
Amazed the gazing rustics ranged around;
And still they gazed, and still the wonder grew
That one small head could carry all he knew.

But past is all his fame. The very spot
Where many a time he triumphed is forgot. —
Near yonder thorn, that lifts its head on high,
Where once the sign-post caught the passing eye,
Low lies that house where nut-brown draughts inspired,
Where graybeard mirth and smiling toil retired,
Where village statesmen talked with looks profound,
And news much older than their ale went round.
Imagination fondly stops to trace
The parlour splendours of that festive place, —
The whitewashed wall; the nicely sanded floor;
The varnished clock that ticked behind the door;
The chest, contrived a double debt to pay,
A bed by night, a chest of drawers by day;
The pictures placed for ornament and use;
The twelve good rules; the royal game of goose;
The hearth, except when winter chilled the day,
With aspen boughs and flowers and fennel gay;
While broken teacups, wisely kept for show,
Ranged o'er the chimney, glistened in a row.

Vain, transitory splendour! could not all
Reprieve the tottering mansion from its fall?
Obscure it silks, nor shall it more impart
An hour's importance to the poor man's heart;
Thither no more the peasant shall repair
To sweet oblivion of his daily care;
No more the farmer's news, the barber's tale
No more the woodman's ballad shall prevail;
No more the smith his dusky brow shall clear,
Relax his ponderous strength, and lean to hear;

The host himself no longer shall be found
Careful to see the mantling bliss go round;
Nor the coy maid, half willing to be prest,
Shall kiss the cup to pass it to the rest.

Yes! let the rich deride, the proud disdain,
These simple blessings of the lowly train;
To me more dear, congenial to my heart,
One native charm, than all the gloss of art.
Spontaneous joys, where nature has its play,
The soul adopts, and owns their first-born sway;
Lightly they frolic o'er the vacant mind,
Unenvied, unmolested, unconfined:
But the long pomp, the midnight masquerade,
With all the freaks of wanton wealth arrayed, —
In these, ere triflers half their wish obtain,
The toiling pleasure sickens into pain;
And e'en while fashion's brightest arts decoy,
The heart, distrusting asks if this be joy.

Ye friends to truth, ye statesmen, who survey
The rich man's joys increas', the poor's decay,
'T is yours to judge, how wide the limits stand
Between a splendid and a happy land.
Proud swells the tide with loads of freighted ore,
And shouting Folly hails them from her shore;
Hoards e'en beyond the miser's wish abound,
And rich men flock from all the world around.
Yet count our gains. This wealth is but a name
That leaves our useful products still the same.
Not so the loss. The man of wealth and pride
Takes up a space that many poor supplied;
Space for his lake, his park's extended grounds,
Space for his horses, equipage, and hounds:
The robe that wraps his limbs in silken sloth
Has robbed the neighbouring fields of half their growth;
His seat, where solitary sports are seen,
Indignant spurns the cottage from the green;

Around the world each needful product flies,
For all the luxuries the world supplies:
While thus the land, adorned for pleasure all,
In barren sp'endour feebly waits the fall.

As some fair female unadorned and plain,
Secure to please while youth confirms her reign,
Slights every borrowed charm that dress supplies,
Nor shares with art the triumph of her eyes,
But when those charms are past,—for charms are frail,—
When time advances, and when lovers fail,
She then shines forth, solicitous to bless,
In all the glaring impotence of dress;
Thus fares the land by luxury betrayed,
In nature's simplest charms at first arrayed,
But verging to decline, its splendours rise,
Its vistas strike, its palaces surprise;
While scourged by famine from the smiling land
The mournful peasant leads his humble band;
And while he sinks, without one arm to save,
The country blooms, —a garden and a grave.

Where then, ah! where shall poverty reside,
To 'scape the pressure of contiguous pride?
If to some common's fenceless limits strayed
He drives his flock to pick the scanty blade,
Those fenceless fields the sons of wealth divide,
And e'en the bare-worn common is denied.
If to the city sped, —what waits him there?
To see profusion that he must not share;
To see ten thousand baneful arts combined
To pamper luxury and thin mankind;
To see each joy the sons of pleasure know
Extorted from his fellow-creature's woe.
Here while the courtier glitters in brocade,
There the pale artist plies the sickly trade;
Here while the proud their long-drawn pomps display,
There the thick gibbet glooms beside the way.

The dome where Pleasure holds the midnight reign,
Here, richly decked, admits the gorgeous train ;
Tumultuous grandeur crowds the blazing square,
The rattling chariots clash, the torches glare.
Sure scenes like these no troubles e'er annoy !
Sure these denote one universal joy !
Are these thy serious thoughts? —Ah, turn thine eyes
Where the poor houseless shivering female lies.
She once, perhaps, in village plenty blest,
Has wept at tales of innocence distrest ;
Her modest looks the cottage might adorn,
Sweet as the primrose peeps beneath the thorn ;
Now lost to all: her friends, her virtue fled,
Near her betrayer's door she lays her head,
And, pinched with cold, and shrinking from the shower,
With heavy heart deplores the luckless hour,
When, idly first ambitious of the town,
She left her wheel and robes of country brown.

Do thine, sweet Auburn, thine, the loveliest train,
Do thy fair tribes participate her pain !
E'en now, perhaps, by cold and hunger led,
At proud men's doors they ask a little bread !

   Ah, no!   To distant climes, a dreary scene,
Where half the convex world intrudes between,
Through torrid tracks with fainting steps they go,
Where wild Altama murmurs to their woe.
Far different there from all that charmed before,
The various terrors of that horrid shore,—
Those blazing suns that dart a downward ray,
And fiercely shed intolerable day ;
Those matted woods where birds forget to sing,
But silent bats in drowsy clusters cling :
Those poisonous fields with rank luxuriance crowned,
Where the dark scorpion gathers death around ;
Where at each step the stranger fears to wake
The rattling terrors of the vengeful snake;

Where crouching tigers wait their hapless prey,
And savage men more murderous still than they;
While oft in whirls the mad tornado fles,
Mingling the ravaged landscape with the skies.
Far different these from every former scene,
The cooling brook, the grassy vested green,
The breezy covert of the warbling grove,
That only sheltered thefts of harmless love.

Good Heaven! what sorrows gloomed that parting day
That called them from their native walks away;
When the poor exiles, every pleasure past,
Hung round the bowers, and fondly looked their last,
And took a long farewell, and wished in vain
For seats like these beyond the western main;
And shuddering still to face the distant deep,
Returned and wept, and still returned to weep.
The good old sire the first prepared to go
To new-found worlds, and wept for other's woe;
But for himself in conscious virtue brave,
He only wished for worlds beyond the grave.
His only daughter, lovelier in her tears,
The fond companion of his helpless years,
Silent went next, neglectful of her charms,
And left a lover's for her father's arms.
With louder plaints the mother spoke her woes,
And blessed the cot where every pleasure rose;
And kissed her thoughtless babes with many a tear,
And clasped them close in sorrow doubly dear;
Whilst her fond husband strove to lend relief
In all the silent manliness of grief.

O Luxury! thou curst by heaven's decree,
How ill exchanged are things like these for thee!
How do thy potions, with insidious joy,
Diffuse their pleasures only to destroy!
Kingdoms by thee, to sickly greatness grown,
Boast of a florid vigour not their own.

At every draught more large and large they grow,
A bloated mass of rank, unwieldy woe;
Till, sapped their strength, and every part unsound,
Down, down they sink, and spread a ruin round.

Even now the devastation is begun,
And half the bu iness of destruction done;
Even now, methinks, as pondering here I stand,
I see the rural virtues leave the land.
Down where yon anchoring vessel spreads the sale
That idly waiting flaps with every gale,
Downward they move, a melancholy band,
Pass from the shore, and darken all the strand.
Contented toil, and hospitable care,
And kind connubial tenderness, are there;
And piety with wishes placed above,
And steady loyalty, and faithful love.
And thou, sweet Poetry, thou loveliest maid,
Still first to fly where sensual joys invade;
Unfit, in these degenerate times of shame,
To catch the heart, or strike for honest fame;
Dear charming nymph, neglected and decried,
My shame in crowds, my solitary pride;
Thou source of all my bliss and all my woe,
That found'st me poor at first and keep'st me so;
Thou guide, by which the nobler arts excel,
Thou nurse of every virtue, fare thee well!
Farewell; and O, where'er thy voice be tried,
On Torno's cliffs, or Pambamarca's side,
Whether where equinoctial fervors glow,
Or winter wraps the polar world in snow,
Still let thy voice, prevailing over time,
Redress the rigors of the inclement clime;
Aid slighted truth with thy persuasive strain;
Teach erring man to spurn the rage of gain;
Teach him, that states of native strength possest
Though very poor, may still be very blest;

That trades proud empire hastes to swift decay,
As ocean sweeps the laboured mole away ;
While self-dependent power can time defy,
As rocks resist the billows and the sky.

OLIVER GOLDSMITH.

⟶L' ALLEGRO⟵

HENCE, loathed melancholy,
  Of Cerberus and blackest Midnight born,
  In Stygian cave forlorn,
'Mongst horrid shapes, and shrieks, and sights
      unholy !
  Find out some uncouth cell,
Where brooding Darkness spreads his jealous wings,
And the night raven sings ;
There under ebon shades, and low-browed rocks,
As ragged as thy locks,
  In Cimmerian desert ever dwell.
But come, thou goddess fair and free,
In heaven ycleped Euphrosyne,
And, by men, heart-easing Mirth ;
Whom lovely Venus, at a birth,
With two sister Graces more,
To ivy-crownéd Bacchus bore ;

Haste thee, nymph, and bring with thee
Jest, and youthful Jollity, —
Quips and cranks and wanton wiles,
Nods and becks and wreathéd smiles,
Such as hang on Hebe's cheek,
And love to live in dimple sleek, —
Sport that wrinkled Care derides,
And Laughter, holding both his sides.
Come ! and trip it, as you go,

9

On the 'ight fantastic toe;
And in thy right hand lead with t' ee
The mountain nymph, sweet Liberty;
And if I give thee honour due,
Mirth, admit me of thy crew,
To live with her, and live with thee,
In unproved pleasures free, —
To hear the lark begin his flight.
And singing startle the dull Night,
From his watch-tower in the skies,
Till the dappled dawn doth rise;
Then to come, in spite of sorrow,
And at my window bid good morrow,
Through the sweet-brier, or the vine,
Or the twisted eglantine;
While the cock with lively din
Scatters the rear of darkness thin,
And to the stack, or baren door,
Stoutly struts his dames before,
Oft lisning how the hounds and horn
Cheerly rouse the slumbering morn,
From the side of some hoar hill
Through the high wood echoing shrill;
Sometimes walking, not unseen,
By hedgerow elms, on hillocks green,
Right against the eastern gate,
Where the great sun begins his state,
Robed in flames, and amber light,
The clouds in thousand liveries dight;
While the ploughman, near at hand,
Whistles o'er the furrowed land,
And the milkmaid singeth blithe,
And the mower whets his scythe,
And every shepherd tells his tale
Under the hawthorn in the dale.
Straight mine eye hath caught new pleasures,
Whilst the landscape round it measures

Russet lawns, and fallow gray,
Where the nibbling flocks do stray, —
Mountains, on whose barren breast
The labouring clouds do often rest, —
Meadows trim with daisies pied,
Shallow brooks ahd rivers wide.
Towers of battlements it sees
Bosomed high on tufted trees,
Where perhaps some beauty lies,
The cynosure of neighbouring eyes.
Hard by, a cottage chimney smokes
From betwixt two aged oaks,
Where Cordon and Thyrsis, met,
Are of their savory dinner set
Of herbs, and other country messes,
Which the neat-handed Phillis dresses:
And then in haste her bower she leaves,
With Thestyl's to bind the sheaves;
Or if the earlier season lead,
To the tanned haycock in the mead.
Sometimes with secure delight
The upland hamlets will invite'
When the merry bell ring round,
At the jocund rebeks sound
To many a youth and many a maid,
Dancing in the checkered shade;
And young and old come forth to play
On a sunshine holiday,
Till the livelong daylight fail;
Then to the spicy nut-brown ale
With stories told of many a feat:
How fairy Mab the junkets eat, —
She was pinched and pulled, she said,
And he, by friar's lantern led;
Tells how the drudging goblin sweat
To earn his cream-bowl duly set,
When in one night, ere glimpse of morn,

His shadowy flail had thrashed the corn
That ten day-labourers could not end ;
Then lies him down the lubber fiend,
And, stretched out all the chimney's length,
Basks at the fire his hairy strength,
And, crop-full, out of doors he flings
Ere the first cock in his matin rings.
Thus done the tales, to bed they creep,
By whispering winds soon lulled asleep.

Towered cities please us then,
And the busy hum of men,
Where throngs of knights and barons bold
In weeds of peace high triumphs hold, —
With store of ladies, whose bright eyes
Rain influence, and judge the prize
Of wit or arms, while both contend
To win her grace whom all commend.
There let Hymen oft appear
In saffron robe, with taper clear,
And pomp and feast and revelry,
With masque, and antique pageantry, —
Such sights as youthful poets dream
On summer eves by haunted stream ;
Then to the well-trod stage anon,
If Jonson's learned sock be on,
Or sweetest Shakespeare, Fancy's child,
Warble his native wood-notes wild.

And ever, against eating cares,
Lap me in soft Lydian airs,
Married to immortal verse, —
Such as the meeting soul may pierce,
In notes with many a winding bout
Of linked sweetness long drawn out,
With wanton heed and giddy cunning
The melting voice through mazes running,

Untwisting all the chains that tie
The hidden soul of harmony, —
That Orpheus' self may heave his head
From golden slumber on a bed
Of heaped Elysian flowers, and hear
Such strains as would have won the ear
Of Pluto, to have quite set free
His half-regained Eurydice.

These delights if thou canst give,
Mirth, with thee I mean to live.

MILTON.

❖SONNET ✚ XXX❖

WHEN to the sessions of sweet silent thought
I summon up remembrance of things past,
I sigh the lack of many a thing I sought,
And with old woes new wail my dear time's waste:
Then can I draw an eye, unused to flow,
For precious friends hid in death's dateless night,
And weep afresh love's long-since-cancelled woe,
And moan the expense of many a vanished sight.
Then can I grieve at grievances foregone,
And heavily from woe to woe tell o'er
The sad account of fore-bemoaned moan,
Which I new pay, as if not paid before;
    But if the while I think on thee, dear friend,
    All losses are restored, and sorrows end.

SHAKESPEARE.

ᐉWHEN✢THE✢LAMP✢IS✢SHATTEREDᐉ

WHEN the lamp is shattered
The light in the dust lies dead;
When the cloud is scattered,
The rainbow's glory is shed.
When the lute is broken,
Sweet tones are remembered not;
When the lips have spoken,
Loved accents are soon forgot.

As music and splendour
Survive not the lamp and the lute,
The heart's echoes render
No song when the spirit is mute, —
No song but sad dirges,
Like the wind through a ruined cell,
Or the mournful surges
That ring the dead seaman's knell.

When hearts have once mingled,
Love first leaves the well-built nest;
The weak one is singled
To endure what it once possessed.
O Love who bewailest
The frailty of all things here,
Why choose you the frailest
For your cradle, your home, and your bier?

Its passions will rock thee
As the storms rock the ravens on high;
Bright reason will mock thee
Like the sun from a wintry sky.
From thy nest every rafter
Will rot, and thine eagle home
Leave thee naked to laughter,
When leaves fall and cold winds come.

PERCY BYSSHE SHELLEY.

➤❖IL✤PENSEROSO❖◄

HENCE, vain deluding joys,
  The brood of Folly without father bred!
  How little you bestead,
Or fill the fixed mind with all your toys!
  Dwell in some idle brain,
And fancies fond with gaudy shapes possess,
As thick and numberless
As the gay motes that people the sunbeams, —
Or likest hovering dreams,
  The fickle pensioners of Morpheus' train.
But hail, thou goddess, sage and holy!
Hail, divinest melancholy!
Whose saintly visage is too bright
To hit the sense of human sight,
And therefore, to our weaker view,
O'erlaid with black, staid Wisdom's hue, —
Black but such as in esteem
Prince Memnon's sister might beseem,
Or that starred Ethiop queen that strove
To set her beauty's prize above
The Sea-Nymphs, and their powers offended.
Yet thou art higher far descended ;
Thee bright-haired Vesta, long of yore,
To solitary Saturn bore, —
His daughter she (in Saturn's reign
Such mixture was not held a stain).
Oft in glimmering bowers and glades
He met her, and in secret shades
Of woody Ida's inmost grove,
While yet there was no fear of Jove.

Come, pensive nun, devout and pure,
Sober, steadfast, and demure,

All in a robe of darkest grain
Flowing with majestic train,
And sable stole of cyprus-lawn
Over thy decent shoulders drawn.
Come, but keep thy wonted state,
With even step, and musing gait,
And looks commercing with the skies,
Thy rapt soul sitting in thine eyes;
There held in holy passion still,
Forget thyself to marble, till
With a sad, leaden, downward cast
Thou fix them on the earth as fast;
And join with the calm Peace, and Quiet, —
Spare Fast, that oft with gods doth diet,
And hears the Muses in a ring
Aye round about Jove's altar sing;
And add to these retired Leisure,
That in trim gardens takes his pleasure:
But first and chiefest, with thee bring
Him that yon soars on golden wing,
Guiding the fiery-wheeled throne, —
The cherub Contemplation;
And the mute Silence hist along,
'Less Philomel will deign a song
In her sweetest, saddest plight,
Smoothing the rugged brow of Night,
While Cynthia checks her dragon yoke
Gently o'er the accustomed oak.
Sweet bird, that shun'st the noise of folly, —
Most musical, most melancholy!
Thee, chantress, oft, the woods among,
I woo, to hear thy even-song.
And, missing thee, I walk unseen
On the dry, smooth-shaven green,
To behold the wandering moon
Riding near the highest noon,
Like one that had been led astray

Through the heaven's wide pathless way;
And oft, as if her head she bowed,
Stooping through a fleecy cloud.
Oft, on a plat of rising ground,
I hear the far-off curfew sound
Over some wide-watered shore,
Swinging slow with sullen roar;
Or if the air will not permit,
Some still removed place will fit,
Where glowing embers through the room
Teach light to counterfeit a gloom, —
Far from all resort of mirth,
Save the cricket on the hearth,
Or the bellman's drowsy charm,
To bless the doors from nightly harm;
Or let my lamp at midnight hour
Be seen in some high lonely tower,
Where I may oft out-watch the Bear
With thrice-great Hermes, or unsphere
The spirit of Plato, to unfold
What worlds or what vast regions hold
The immortal mind that hath forsook
Her mansion in this fleshy nook;
And of those demons that are found
In fire, air, flood, or under ground,
Whose power hath a true consent
With planet or with element.
Sometimes let gorgeous Tragedy
In sceptred pall come sweeping by,
Presenting Thebes, or Pelops' line,
Or the tales of Troy divine,
Or what (though rare) of later age
Ennobled hath the buskined stage.

But, O sad Virgin, that thy power
Might raise Musæus from his bower!
Or bid the soul of Orpheus sing

10

Such notes as, warbled to the string,
Drew iron tears from Pluto's cheek,
And made hell grant what love did seek!
Or call up him that left half told
The story of Cambuscan bold, —
Of Camball, and of Algarsife, —
And who had Canacé to wife,
That owned the virtuous ring and glass, —
And of the wondrous horse of brass,
On which the Tartar king did ride!
And, if aught else great bards beside
In sage and solemn tunes have sung, —
Of tourneys and of trophies hung,
Of forests, and enchantments drear
Where more is meant than meets the ear.

Thus, Night, oft see me in my pale career,
Till civil-suited Morn appear, —
Not tricked and frounced, as she was wont
With the Attic boy to hunt,
But kerchiefed in a comely cloud,
While rocking winds are piping loud,
Or ushered with a shower still
When the gust hath blown his fill,
Ending in the rustling leaves,
With minute drops from off the eaves.
And when the sun begins to fling
His flaring beams, me, goddess, bring,
To archéd walks of twilight groves,
And shadows brown, that Sylvan loves,
Of pine, or monumental oak,
Where the rude axe with heavéd stroke
Was never heard the Nymphs to daunt,
Or fright them from their hallowed haunt.
There in close covert by some brook,
Where no profaner eye may look,
Hide me from day's garish eye,

While the bee with honeyed thigh,
That at her flowery work doth sing,
And the waters murmuring
With such consort as they keep,
Entice the dewy-feathered Sleep;
And let some strange mysterious dream
Wave at his wings, in airy stream
Of lively portraiture displayed.
Softly on my eyelids laid:
And, as I wake, sweet music breathe
Above, about, or underneath,
Sent by some Spirit for mortals good,
Or the unseen Genius of the wood.

But let my due feet never fail
To walk the studious cloisters pale,
And love the high embowéd roof,
With antic pillars massy proof,
And storied windows, richly dight,
Casting a dim religious light.
There let the pealing organ blow
To the full-voiced quire below,
In service high and anthems clear,
As may with sweetness through mine ear,
Dissolve me into ecstasies,
And bring all heaven before mine eyes.

And may at last my weary age
Find out the peaceful hermitage,
The hairy gown and mossy cell,
Where I may sit and rightly spell
Of every star that heaven doth shew,
And every herb that sips the dew,
Till old experience do attain
To something like prophetic strain.
These pleasures, Melancholy, give,
And I with thee will choose to live.

Milton.

THE SOLITARY REAPER

BEHOLD her, single in the field,
  Yon solitary Highland lass!
Reaping and singing by herself;
  Stop here or gently pass!
Alone she cuts and binds the grain,
And sings a melancholy strain;
Oh listen! for the vale profound
Is overflowing with the sound.

No nightingale did ever chant
  More welcome notes to weary bands
Of travellers in some shady haunt,
  Among Arabian sands;
A voice so thrilling ne'er was heard
In spring time from the cuckoo bird,
Breaking the silence of the seas
Among the farthest Hebrides.

Will no one tell me what she sings?
  Perhaps the plaintive numbers flow
For old, unhappy, far-off things,
  And battles long ago;
Or is it some more humble lay,
Familiar matter of to-day?
Some natural sorrow, loss, or pain,
That has been, or may be again?

Whate'er the theme the maiden sang
  As if her song could have no ending;
I saw her singing at her work
  And o'er her sickle bending; —
I listened motionless and still;
And, as I mounted up the hill,
The music in my heart I bore
Long after it was heard no more.

WILLIAM WORDSWORTH.

ODE TO AUTUMN

SEASON of mists and mellow fruitfulness!
  Close bosom-friend of the maturing sun!
Conspiring with him how to load and bless
  With fruit the vines that round the thatch-eves run—
To bend with apples the mossed cottage trees,
  And fill all fruit with ripeness to the core—
    To swell the gourd, and plump the hazel shells
With a sweet kernel—to set budding more
And still more, later flowers for the bees,
Until they think warm days will never cease,
    For Summer has o'er-brimmed their clammy cells.

Who hath not seen thee oft amid thy store?
  Sometimes whoever seeks abroad may find
Thee sitting careless on a granary floor,
  Thy hair soft-lifted by the winnowing wind;
Or on a half-reaped furrow sound asleep,
  Drowsed with the fume of poppies, while thy hook
    Spares the next swath and all its twinéd flowers;
And sometimes like a gleaner thou dost keep
  Steady thy laden dead across a brook;
  Or by a cider press, with patient look,
    Thou watchest the last oozings, hours by hours.

Where are the songs of Spring? Ay, where are they?
  Think not of them—thou hast thy music too:
Where barred clouds bloom the soft-dying day,
  And touch the the stubble-plains with rosy hue:
Then in a wailful choir the small gnats mourn
  Among the river shallows, borne aloft
    Or sinking, as the light wind lives or dies;
And full-grown lambs loud bleat from hilly bourn;
  Hedge-crickets sing; and now with treble soft
  The redreast whistles from a garden-croft,
    And gathering swallows twitter in the skies.

JOHN KEATS.

❖CHORUS✢FROM✢"ATALANTA"❖

WHEN the hounds of spring are on winter's traces,
  The mother of months in meadow or plain
Fills the shadows and windy places
  With lisp of leaves and ripple of rain;
And the brown bright nightingale amorous
Is half assuaged for Itylus,
For the Thracian ships and the foreign faces,
  The tongueless vigil, and all the pain.

Come with bows bent and with emptying of quivers,
  Maiden most perfect, lady of light,
With a noise of winds and many rivers,
  With a clamour of waters, and with might;
Bind on thy sandals, O thou most fleet,
Over the splendour and speed of thy feet;
For the faint east quickens, the wan west shivers,
  Round the feet of the day and the feet of the night.

Where shall we find her, how shall we sing to her,
  Fold our hands round her knees and cling?
Oh that man's heart were as fire and could spring to her,
  Fire or the strength of the streams that spring!
For the stars and the winds are unto her
As raiment, as song of the harp-player;
For the risen stars and the fallen cling to her,
  And the south-west wind and the west wind sing.

For winter's rains and ruins are over,
  And all the season of snows and sins;
The days dividing lover and lover,
  The light that loses, the night that wins;
And time remembered is grief forgotten,
And frosts are slain and flowers begotten,
And in green underwood and cover
  Blossom by blossom the spring begins.

The full streams feed on flower of rushes,
　Ripe grasses trammel a travelling foot,
The faint fresh flame of the young year flushes
　From leaf to flower and from flower to fruit;
And fruit and leaf are as gold and fire,
And the oat is heard above the lyre,
And the hoofèd heel of a satyr crushes
　The chestnut-husk at the chestnut-root.

ALGERNON CHARLES SWINBURNE.

➤✳LIFE✳◄

LIFE! I know not what thou art,
But know that thou and I must part;
And when, or how, or when we met,
I own to me 's a secret yet.
But this I know: when thou art fled,
Where'er they lay these limbs, this head,
No clod so valuless shall be
As all that then remaine of me.

Life! we've been long together
Through pleasant and through cloudy weather;
'Tis hard to part when friends are dear;
Perhaps 'twill cost a sigh, a tear
　Then steal away, give little warning,
　　Choose thine own time;
Say not Good-night, —but in some brighter clime
　Bid me Good-morning.

ANNA LETITIA BARBAULD.

⇥✴FAREWELL✴⇤

FAREWELL ! but whenever you welcome the hour
That awakens the night-song of mirth in yotr bower,
Then think of your friend who once welcomed it too,
And forgot his own griefs to be happy with you.
His griefs may return, not a hope may remain
Of the few that have brightened his pathway of pain,
But he ne'er will forget the short vision that threw
Its enchantment around him while lingering with you ;

And still on that evening, when pleasure fills up
To the highest top-sparkle each heart and each cup,
Where'er my path lies, be it gloomy or bright,
My soul happy friends ! shall be with you that night—
Shall join in your revels, your sports, and your wiles,
And return to me beaming all o'er with your smiles ;
Too blest if it tells me that, 'mid the gay cheer,
Some kind voice had murmured, "I wish he were here! "

Let Fate do her worst, there are relies of joy,
Bright dreams of the past, which she cannot destroy !
Which come in the night-time os sorrow and care,
And bring back the features that joy used to wear.
Long, long be my heart with such memories filled !
Like the vase in which roses have once been distilled ;
You may break, you may ruin the vase if you will,
But the scent of the roses will hang round it still.

THOMAS MOORE.

→✷HE✦WHO✦DIED✦AT✦AZAN✦←

He who died at Azan sends
This to comfort all his friends;

Faithful friends! It lies, I know,
Pale and white and cold as snow:
And ye say, " Abdullah's dead!"
Weeping at the feet and head
I can see your falling tears,
I can hear your sighs and prayers;
Yet I smile and whisper this:
I am not the thing you kiss.
Cease your tears and, and let it lie;
It was mine—it was not I.

Sweet friends! what the women lave
For i's last bed of the grave,
Is a hut which I am quitting,
Is a garment no more fitting,
Is a cage from which, at last,
Like a hawk my soul hath pas ed;
Love the inmate, not the room,
The wearer, not the garb; the plume
Of the falcon, not the bars
That kept him from the splendid stars!

Loving friends! be wise, and dry
Straightway every weeping eye.
What ye lift upon the bier
Is not worth a wistful tear.
'Tis an empty sea-shell, one
Out of which the pearl has gone.
The shell is broken, it lies there;
The pearl, the all, the soul, is here.

'Tis an earthern jar whose lid
Allah sealed, the while it hid
That treasure of his treasury,
A mind that loved him : let it lie!
Let the shard be earth's once more,
Since the gold shines in the store!

Allah glorious! Allah good!
Now Thy world is understood;
Now the long, long wonder ends!
Yet ye weep, my erring friends,
While the man whom ye call dead,
In unspoken bliss instead,
Lives and loves you; lost, 'tis true,
By such light as shines for you;
But, in the light you cannot see,
Of unfulfilled felicity,
In enlarging paradise
Lives a life that never dies.

Farewell, friends! yet not farewell—
Where I am ye too shall dwell.
I am gone before your face,
A moment's time, a little space.
When you come where I have stept,
Ye will wonder why ye wept;
Ye will know, by wise love taught,
That here is all and there is naught.
Weep a while, if ye are fain,
Sunshine still must follow rain,
Only not at death; for death,
Now I know, is that first breath
Which our souls draw when we enter
Life which is of all life centre.

Be ye certain, all seems love,
Viewed from Allah's throne above!
Be ye stout of heart and come

, Bravely onward to your home!
  La Allah illa Allah! yea!
  Thou love divine! Thou love alway!

He that died at Azan gave
This to those who made his grave.

EDWIN ARNOLD.

→✳ODE ÷ TO ÷ A ÷ GRECIAN ÷ URN✳←

THOU still unfaded bride of quietness!
  Thou foster-child of silence and slow time,
Sylvan historian, who canst thus express
  A flowery tale more sweetly than our rhyme!
What leaf-fringed legend haunts about thy shape
  Of deities or mortals, or of the both,
    In Tempe or the dales of Arcady?
  What men or gods are these? what maidens loath?
What mad pursuit? What struggle to escape?
  What pipes and timbrels? What wild ecstasy?

Heard melodies are sweet, but those unheard
  Are sweeter; therefore, ye soft pipes play on—
Not to the sensual ear, but more endeared,
  Pipe to the spirit ditties of no tone!
Fair youth beneath the trees, thou canst not leave
  Thy song, nor ever can those trees be bare;
    Bold lover, never, never canst thou kiss,
Though winning near the goal; yet do not grieve—
    She cannot fade, though thou hast not thy bliss;
  For ever wilt thou love, and she be fair!

Ah, happy, happy boughs! that cannot shed
  Your leaves, nor ever bid the spring adieu:
And happy melodist, unwearied,
  For ever piping songs for ever new;

More happy love! more happy, happy love!
  For ever warm and still to be enjoyed,
    For ever panting and for ever young;
All breathing human passion far above,
  That leaves a heart high sorrowful and cloyed,
    A burning forehead and a parching tongue.

Who are these coming to the sacrifice?
  To what green altar, O mysterious priest,
Lead'st thou that heifer lowing at the skies,
  And all her silken flanks with garlands drest?
What little town by river or sea-shore,
  Or mountain-built with peaceful citadel,
    Is emptied of its folk, this pious morn?
And, little town, thy streets for evermore
  Will silent be; and not a soul, to tell
    Why thou art desolate, can e'er return.

O Attic shape!   Fair attitude! with brede
  Of marble men and maidens overwrough',
With forest branches and the trodden weed!
  Thou, silent form! dost tease us out of thought,
As doth eternity.   Cold pastoral!
  When old age shall this generation waste,
    Thou shalt remain. in midst of other woe
Than ours, a friend to man, to whom thou say'st
"Beauty is truth, truth beauty,"—that is all
  Ye know on earth, and all ye need to know.
JOHN KEATS

❊THE BABY❊

On parents' knees, a naked, new-born child,
Weeping thou sat'st when all around thee smiled:
So live, that, sinking in thy last long sleep,
Thou then mayst smile while all around thee weep.
From the Sanscrit of CALIDASA, by
SIR WILLIAM JONES.

→❊M'PHERSON'S✢FAREWELL❊←

"FAREWELL, ye dungeons dark and strong,
  The wretch's destinie!
M'Pherson's time will not be long
  On yonder gallows-tree."
    Sae rantingly, sae wantingly,
      Sae dauntingly gaed he;
    He play'd a spring, and danc'd it round,
      Below the gallows-tree.

"O, what is death but parting breath?
  On many a bloody plain
I've dar'd his face and in this place
  I scorn him yet again!

"Untie these bands from off my hands,
  And bring to me my sword;
And there 's no a man in all Scotland,
  But I'll brave him at a word.

"I've liv'd a life of sturt and strife;
  I die by treacherie:
It burns my heart I must depart,
  And not avengéd be.

"Now farewell light, thou sunshine bright,
  And all beneath the sky!
May coward shame disdain his name,
  The wretch that dares not die!"
    Sae rantingly, sae wantonly,
      Sae dauntingly gaed he;
    He play'd a spring, and danc'd it round,
      Below the gallows-tree.

ROBERT BURNS.

➤✳MINSTREL'S·SONG✳◄

OH, sing unto my roundelay!
  Oh, drop the briny tear with me!
Dance no more at holiday;
  Like a running river be.
      My love is dead,
      Gone to his death-bed,
      All under the willow-tree.

Black his hair as the winter night,
  White his neck as the summer snow'
Ruddy his face as the morning light;
  Cold he lies in the grave below.

Sweet his tongue as the throstle's note;
  Quick in dance as thought can be:
Deft his tabor, cudgel stout;
  Oh, he lies by the willow-tree!

Hark! the raven flaps his wing
  In the briered dell below;
Hark! the death-owl loud doth sing
  To the nightmares as they go.

See! the white moon shines on high;
  Whiter is my true loves shroud,
Whiter than the morning sky,
  Whiter than the evening cloud.

Here upon my true-love's grave
  Shall the barren flowers be laid,
Nor one holy saint to save
  All the coldness of a maid.

With my hands I'll bind the briers
  Round his holy corse to gre;
Ouphant fairy, light your fires;
  Here my body still shall be.

Come, with acorn-cup and thorn,
  Drain my heart's blood all away;
Life and all its good I scorn,
  Dance by night, and feast by day.
    My love is dead,
    Gone to his death-bed,
    All under the willow-tree.

THOMAS CHATTERTON.

➤✳STANZAS·TO·AUGUSTA✳◄

THOUGH the day of my destiny's over,
  And the star of my fate hath declined,
Thy soft heart refused to discover
  The faults which so many could find;
Though thy soul with my grief was acquainted,
  It shrunk not to share it with me,
And the love which my spirit hath painted
  It never hath found but in thee.

Then when nature around me is smiling,
  The last smile that answers to mine,
I do not believe it beguiling,
  Because it reminds me of thine:
And when winds are at war with the ocean,
  As the breasts I believed in with me,
If their billows excite an emotion,
  It is that they bear me from thee.

Though the rock of my last hope is shivered,
 And its fragments are sunk in the wave,
Though I feel that my soul is delivered
 To pain—it shall not be its slave.
There is many a pang to pursue me:
 They may crush, but they shall not contemn—
They may torture, but shall not subdue me—
 'Tis of thee that I think, not of them.

Though human, thou didst not deceive me,
 Though woman, thou didst not forsake,
Though loved, thou foreborest to grieve me,
 Though slandered, thou never couldst shake,
Though trusted, thou didst not disclaim me,
 Though parted, it was not to fly,
Though watchful, 'twas not to defame me,
 Nor mute that the world might belie.

Yet I blame not the world, nor despise it,
 Nor the war of the many with one;
If my soul was not fitted to prize it,
 'Twas folly not sooner to shun;
And if dearly that error hath cost me,
 And more than I once could forsee,
I have found that, whatever it lost me,
 It could not deprive me of thee.

From the wreck of the past which hath perished
 Thus much I at least may recall,
It hath taught me that what I most cherished
 Deserved to be dearest of all.
In the desert a fountain is springing,
 In the wild waste there still is a tree,
And a bird in the solitude singing,
 Which speaks to my spirit of thee.

GEORGE GORDON BYRON.

❖LOCHINVAR❖

OH, young Lochinvar is come out of the west:
Through all the wide border his steed was the best:
And save his good broad-sword he weapon had none;
He rode all unarmed, and he rode all alone.
So faithful in love, and so dauntless in war,
There never was knight like the young Lochinvar.

He staid not for brake, and he stopped not for stone;
He swam the Esk river where ford there was none;
But, ere he alighted at Netherby gate,
The bride had consented, the gallant came late:
For a laggard in love, and a dastard in war,
Was to wed the fair Ellen of brave Lochinvar.

So boldly he entered the Netherby hall,
'Mong bridesmen, and kinsmen, and brothers, and all;
Then spoke the bride's father, his hand on his sword,
(For the poor craven bridegroom said never a word,)
"O come ye in peace here, or come ye in war,
Or to dance at our bridal, young Lord Lochinvar?"

"I long wooed your daughter, my suit you denied;
Love swells the Solway, but ebbs like its tide;
And now I am come, with this lost love of mine,
To lead but one measure, drink one cup of wine;
There are maidens in Scotland more lovely by far,
That would gladly be bride to the young Lochinvar."

The bride kissed the goblet, the knight took it up;
He quaffed off the wine, and he threw down the cup.
She looked down to blush, and she looked up to sigh
With a smile on her lips, and a tear in her eye.
He took her soft hand, ere her mother could bar,
"Now tread we a measure!" said young Lochinvar.

So stately his form, and so lovely her face,
That never a hall such a galliard did grace ;
While her mother did fret and her father did fume,
And the bridegroom stood dangling his bonnet and
   plume ;
And the bride-maidens whispered, " 'Twere better by
   far
To have matched our fair cousin with young Lochin-
var. "

One touch to her hand, and one word to her ear,
When they reached the hall door and the charger stood
   near ;
So light to the croupe the fair lady he swung,
So light to the saddle before her he sprung !
"She is won ! we are gone, over bank, bush, and scaur ;
They'll have fleet steeds that follow, " quoth young
   Lochinvar.

There was mounting 'mong Græmes of the Netherby
   clan ;
Forsters, Fenwicks, and Musgraves, they rode and they
   ran :
There was racing, and chasing, on Cannobie Lee,
But the lost bride of Netherby ne'er did they see.
So daring in love, and so dauntless in war,
Have ye e'er heard of gallant like young Lochinvar?
                                        SIR WALTER SCOTT.

➤✷DEAD✧FRIENDS✷◄

,Tis sweet, as year by year we lose
  Friends out of sight, in faith to muse
  How grows in Paradise our store.
   - Burial of the Dead.   JOHN KEBLE.

→✳ISLES✢OF✢GREECE✳←

FROM "DON JUAN," CANTO III.

THE isles of Greece, the isles of Greece!
  Where burning Sappho loved and sung, —
Where grew the arts of war and peace, —
  Where Delos rose, and Phœbus sprung!
Eternal summer gilds them yet;
But all, except their sun, is set.

The Scian, and the Teian muse,
  The hero's harp, the lover's lute,
Have found the fame your shores refuse;
  Their place of birth alone is mute
To sounds which echo farther west
Than your sires' "I-lands of rhe Blest."

The mountains look on Marathon,
  And Marathon looks on the sea;
And musing there an hour alone,
  I dreamed that Greece might still be free;
For, standing on the Persians' grave,
I could not deem myself a slave.

A king sat on the rocky brow
  Which looks o'er sea-born Salamis;
And ships by thous nds lay below,
  And men in nations, —all were his!
He counted them at break of day, —
And when the sun set, where were they!

And where are they! and where art thou,
  My country? On thy voiceless shore
The heroic lay is tuneless now, —
  The heroic bosom beats no more!

And must thy lyre, so long divine,
Degenerate into hands like mine?

'Tis something, in the death of fame,
    Though linked among a fettered race,
To feel at least a patriot's shame,
    Even as I sing, suffuse my face;
For what is left the poet here?
For Greeks blush, —for Greece a tear.

Must we but weep o'er days more blest?
    Must we but blush? —our fathers bled.
Earth! render back from out thy breast
    A remnant of our Spartan dead!
Of the three hundred, grant but three
To make a new Thermopylœ!

What, silent still! and silent all?
    Ah, no! the voices of the dead?
Sound like a distant torrent's fall,
    And answer, " Let one living head,
But one, arise, — we come, we come!"
'Tis but the living who are dumb.

In vain, —in vain; strike other chords;
    Fill high the cup with Samian wine!
Leave battles to the Turkish hordes,
    And shed the blood of Scio's vine!
Hark! rising to the ignoble call,
How answers each bold Bacchanal?

You have the Pyrrhic dance as yet, —
    Where is the Pyrrhic phalaux gone?
Of two such lessons, why forget
    The nobler and the manlier one?
You have the letters Cadmus gave, —
Think ye he meant them for a slave;

Fill high the bowl with Samian wine!
    We will not think of themes like these!

It made Anacreon's song divine:
  He served, but served Polycrates —
A tyrant; but our masters then
Were still, at least, our countrymen.

The tyrant of the Chersonese
  Was freedom's best and bravest friend;
That tyrant was Miltiades!
  O that the present hour would lend
Another despot of the kind!
Such chains as his were sure to bind.

Fill high the bowl with Samian wine!
  On Suli's rock and Parga's shore
Exists the remnant of a line
  Such as the Doric mothers bore;
And there perhaps some seed is sown
The Heracleidan blood might own.

Trust not for freedom to the Franks, —
  They have a king who buys and sells:
In native words, and native ranks,
  The only hope of courage dwells;
But Turkish force, and Latin fraud,
Would break your shield, however broad.

Place me on Sunium's marble steep,
  Where nothing, save the waves and I,
May hear our mutual murmurs sweep:
  There, swan-like, let me sing and die.
A land of slaves shall ne'er be mine, —
Dash down yon cup of Samian wine!

GEORGE GORDON BYRON.

AVE MARIA

AVE MARIA ! Maiden mild !
Listen to a maiden's prayer:
Thou canst hear though from the wild,
Thou canst save amid despair.
Safe may we sleep beneath thy care,
Though banished, outcast, and reviled—
Maiden ! hear a maiden's prayer;
Mother, hear a suppliant child ! —
Ave Maria !

Ave Maria ! undefiled !
The flinty couch we now must share
Shall seem with down of eider piled
If thy protection hover there.
The musky cavern's heavy air
Shall breathe a balm if thou hast smiled;
Then, Maiden ! hear a maiden's prayer !
Mother, list a suppliant child !—
Ave Maria !

Ave Maria ! stainless styled !
Foul demons of the earth and air,
From their wonted haunt exiled,
Shall flee before thy presence fair.
We bow us to our lot of care,
Beneath thy guidance reconciled;
Hear for a maid a maiden's prayer !
And for a father hear a child !
Ave Maria !

SIR WALTER SCOTT.

➤✵UNDER ÷ THE ÷ GREENWOOD ÷ TREE✵←

UNDER the greenwood tree
Who loves to lie with me,
And tune his merry note
Unto the sweet bird's throat,
Come hither, come hither, come hither ;
Here shall he see
No enemy
But Winter and rough weather.

Who doth ambition shun
And loves to live i' the sun,
Seeking the food he eats,
And pleased with what he gets
Come hither, come hither, come hither ;
Here shall he see
No enemy
But Winter and rough weather.

SHAKESPEARE.

➤✵EASTER✵←

I got me flowers to strew they way—
    I got me boughs off many a tree ;
But thou wast up by break of day,
    And brought'st thy sweets along with thee.

The sun arising in the east,
    Though he give light and th' east perfume,
If they should offer to contest,
    With Thy arising, they presume.

Can there be any day but this,
    Though many suns to shine endeavour?
We count three hundred, but we miss —
    There is but one, and that one ever.

GEORGE HERBERT.

AMONG THE BEAUTIFUL PICTURES

AMONG the beautiful pictures
  That hang on memory's wall,
Is one of a dim old forest,
  That seemeth best of all.
Not for its gnarled oaks olden,
  Dark with the misletoe;
Not for the violets golden
  That sprinkle the vale below;
Not for the milk-white lilies
  That lean from the fragrant ledge,
Coquetting all day with the sunbeams,
  And stealing their golden edge;
Not for the vines on the upland,
  Where the bright red berries rest;
Nor the pinks, nor the pale, sweet cowslip,
  It seemeth to me the best.

I once had a little brother
  With eyes that were dark and deep;
In the lap of that old green forest
  He lieth in peace asleep;
Light as the dew on the thistle,
  Free as the winds that blow,
We roved there the beautiful summers,
  The summers of long ago;
But his feet on the hills grew weary,
  And one of the autumn eves
I made for my little brother
  A bed of yellow leaves.

Sweetly his pale arms folded
  My neck in a meek embrace,
As the light of immortal beauty
  Silently covered his face;

And when the arrows of sunset
  Lodged in the tree-tops bright,
He fell, in a saint like beauty,
  Asleep by the gates of light.
Therefore, of all the pictures
  That hang on memory's wall,
The one of the dim old forest
Seemeth the best of all.

ALICE CARY.

➤SONG➤

WHEN I am dead, my dearest,
  Sing no sad songs for me;
Plant thou no roses at my head,
  Nor shady cypress-tree:
Let the green grass be above me
  With showers and dewdrops wet;
And if thou wilt, remember,
  And if thou wilt, forget.

I shall not see the shadows,
  I shall not feel the rain;
I shall not hear the nightingale
  Sing on, as if in pain;
And dreaming through the twilight
  That doth not rise nor set,
Haply I may remember,
  And haply may forget.

CHRISTINA G. ROSSETTI.

❖MY❖MOTHER'S❖PICTURE❖

O THAT those lips had language! Life has passed
With me but roughly since I heard them last.
Those lips are thine, —thy own sweet smile I see,
The same that oft in childhood solaced me;
Voice only fails, else how distinct they say,
"Grieve not, my child; chase all thy fears away!"
The meek intelligence of those dear eyes
(Blest be the art that can immortalise, —
The art that baffles time's tyrannic claim
To quench it!) here shines on me the same.
  Faithful remembrancer of one so dear!
O welcome guest, though unexpected here!
Who bid'st me honour with an artless song'
Affectionate, a mother lost so long·
I will obey, —not willingly alone,
But gladly, as the precept were her own;
And, while that face renews my filial grief,
Fancy shall weave a charm for my relief, —
Shall steep me in Elysian revery,
A momentary dream that thou art she.

  Could time, his flight reversed, restore the hours
When, playing with my vesture's tissued flowers, —
The violet, the pink and jessamine, —
I pricked them into paper with a pin,
(And thou wast happier than myself the while—
Wou dst softly speak, and stroke my head and smile,'—
Could those few pleasant days again appear,
Might one wish bring them, would I bring them here?
I would not trust my heart, —the dear delight
Seems so to be desired, perhaps I might
But no, —what here we call our life is such,
So little to be loved, and thou so much,
That I should ill requite thee to constrain

Thy unbound spirit into bonds again.
   Thou—as a gallant bark, from Albion's coast,
(The storms all weathered and the ocean crossed,)
Shoots into port at some well-havened isle,
Where spices breathe and brighter seasons smile; ·
There sits quiescent on the floods, that show
Her beauteous form reflected clear below,
While airs impregnated with incense play
Around her, fanning light her streamers gay, —
So thou, with sails how swift! hast reached the shore
" Where tempests never beat nor billows roar,"
And thy loved consort on the dangerous tide
Of life long since has anchored by thy side.
But me, scarce hoping to attain that rest,
Always from port withheld, always distressed, —
Me howling blasts drive devious, tempest-tossed,
Sails ripped, seams opening wide, and compass lost;
And day by day some current's thwarting force
Sets me more distant from a prosperous course.
Yet O, the thought that thou art safe, and he! —
That thought is joy, arrive what may to me.
My boast is not that I deduce my birth
From loins enthroned, and rulers of the earth;
But higher for my proud pretensions rise, —
The son of parents passed into the skies.
And now, farewell!—Time, unrevoked, has run
His wonted course; yet what I wished is done.
By contempla ion's help, not sought in vain,
I seem to have lived my childhood o'er again, —
To have renewed the joys that once were mine,
Without the sin of violating thine;
And, while the wings of fancy still are free,
And I can view this mimic show of thee,
Time has but half succeeded in his theft, —
Thyself removed, thy power to soothe me left.
WILLIAM COWPER

→✳MAY✜TIME✳←

FROM "THE CUCKOO and the NIGHTINGALE."

THE God of love,—*ah, benedicite !*
How mighty and how great a lord is he!
For he of low hearts can make high; of high
He can make low, and unto death bring nigh;
And hard hearts, he can make them kind and free.

In brief, the whole of what he will he may;
Against him dare not any wight say nay;
To humble or afflict whome'er he will,
To gladden or to grieve, he hath like skill;
But most his might he sheds on the eve of May.

For every true heart, gentle heart and free,
That with him is, or thinketh so to be,
Now, against May, shall have some stirring,—whether
To joy, or be it some mourning: never,
At another time, methinks, in like degree.

For now, when they may hear the small birds' song,
And see the budding leaves the branches throng,
This into their remembrance doth bring
All kinds of pleasure, mixed with sorrowing;
And longing for sweet thoughts that ever long.

And of that longing heaviness doth come,
Whence oft great sickness grows of heart and home;
Sick are they all for lack of this desire;
And thus in May their hearts are set on fire,
So that they burn forth in great martyrdom.

GEOFFREY CHAUCER.

→✳THE✜DAY✜IS✜DONE✳←

THE day is done, and the darkness
　Falls from the wings of Night,
As a feather is wafted downward
　From an Eagle in his flight.

I see the lights of the village
　Gleam through the rain and the mist,
And a feeling of sadness comes o'er me,
　That my soul cannot resist;

A feeling of sadness and longing,
　That is not akin to pain,
And resembles sorrow only
　As the mist resembles rain.

Come, read to me some poem,
　Some simple and heartfelt lay,
That shall soothe this restless feeling,
　And banish the thoughts of day.

Not from the grand old masters,
　Not from the bards sublime,
Whose distant footsteps echo
　Through the corridors of time.

For, like the strains of martial music,
　Their mighty thoughts suggest
Life's endless toil and endeavour;
　And to-night I long for rest.

Read from some humbler poet,
　Whose songs gushed from his heart,
As showers from the clouds of summer,
　Or tears from the eyelids start;

Who through long days of labour,
  And nights devoid of ease,
Still heard in his soul the music
  Of wonderful melodies.

Such songs have power to quiet
  The restless pulse of care,
And come like the benediction
  That follows after prayer.

Then read from the treasured volume
  The poem of thy choice,
· And lend to the rhyme of the poet
  The beauty of thy voice.

And the night shall be filled with music,
  And the cares, that infest the day,
Shall fold their tents, like the Arabs,
  And as silently steal away.

HENRY WADSWORTH LONGFELLOW.

⁘ASPECTA·MEDUSA⁘

ANDROMEDA, by Perseus saved and wed,
Hankered each day to see the Gorgon's head :
Till o'er a fount he held it, bade her lean,
And mirrored in the wave was safely seen
That death she lived by.

      Let not thine eyes know
Any forbidden thing itself although
It once should save as well as kill : but be
Its shadow upon life enough for thee.

DANTE GABRIEL ROSSETTI.

→✳AN✳APOLOGY✳←

PROLOGUE TO "THE EARTHLY PARADISE."

Of Heaven or Hell I have no power to sing,
I cannot ease the burden of your fears,
Or make quick-coming death a little thing,
Or bring again the pleasure of past years,
Nor for my words shall ye forget your tears,
Or hope again for aught that I can say,
The idle singer of an empty day.

But rather, when aweary of your mirth,
From full hearts still unsatisfied ye sigh,
And, feeling kindly unto all the earth,
Grudge every minute as it passes by,
Made the more mindful that the sweet days die,—
Remember me a little then, I pray
The idle singer of an empty day.

The heavy trouble, the bewildering care
That weighs us down who live and earn our bread,
These idle verses have no power to bear;
So let me sing of names remembered,
Because they, living out, can ne'er be dead,
Or long time take their memory quite away
From us poor singers of an empty pay.

Dreamer of dreams, born out my due time,
Why should I strive to set the crooked straight?
Let it suffice me that my murmuring rhyme
Beats with light wing against the ivory gate,
Telling a tale not too importunate
To those who in the sleepy region stay,
Lulled by the singer of an empty day.

Folk say, a wizard to a northern king
At Christmas-tide such wondrous things did show,
That through one window men beheld the spring,
And through another saw the summer glow,
And through a third the fruited vines arow,
While still, unheard, but in its wonted way,
Piped the drear wind of that December day.

So with this Earthly Paradise it is,
If ye will read aright, and pardon me,
Who strive to build a shadowy isle of bliss
Midmost the beating of the steely sea,
Where tossed about all hearts of men must be;
Whose ravening monsters mighty men shall slay,
Not the poor singer of an empty day.

WILLIAM MORRIS.

❖ EARLY · FRIENDSHIP ❖

THE half-seen memories of childish days,
   When pains and pleasures lightly came and went;
   The sympathies of boy-hood rashly spent
In fearful wanderings through forbidden ways!
The vague but manly wish to tread the maze
   Of life to noble ends ; whereon intent,
   Asking to know for what man here was sent,
The bravest heart must often pause, and gaze;
The firm resolve to seek the chosen end
   Of manhood's judgement, cautious and mature:
Each of these viewless bonds binds friend to friend
   With strength no selfish purpose can secure ;
My happy lot is this, that all attend
   That friendship which first came, and which shall last
     endure.

AUBREY DE VERE.

THE PILLAR OF THE CLOUD

LEAD, kindly Light, amid the encircling gloom,
    Lead thou me on !
The night is dark, and I am far from home, —
    Lead thou me on !
Keep thou my feet; I do not ask to see
The distant scene, —one step enough for me.

I was not ever thus, nor prayed that thou
    Shouldst lead me on :
I loved to choose and see my path, but now
    Lead thou me on !
I loved the garish day, and, spite of fears,
Pride ruled my will : remember not past years.

So long thy power hath blessed me, sure it still
    Will lead me on ;
O'er moor and fen, o'er crag and torrent, till
    The night is gone ;
And with the morn those angel faces smile
Which I have loved long since, and lost awhile.

              JOHN, CARDINAL NEWMAN

MOTHER-LOVE

A mother's love, —how sweet the name !
    What is a mother's love ? —
A noble, pure, and tender flame,
    Enkindled from above,
To bless a heart of earthly mould ;
The warmest love that can grow cold ;—
    This is a mother's love.

A Mother's Love.   JAMES MONTGOMERY.

→✳INCIDENT✳OF✳THE✳FRENCH✳CAMP✳←

You know we French stormed Ratisbon:
　A mile or so away,
On a little mound, Napoleon
　Stood on our storming-day;
With neck out-thrust, you fancy how,
　Legs wide, arms locked behind,
As if to balance the prone brow,
　Oppressive with its mind.

Just as perhaps he mused, " My plans
　That soar, to earth may fall,
Let once my army-leader Lannes
　Waver at yonder wall,"—
Out 'twixt the battery-smokes there flew
　A rider, bound on bound
Full-galloping; nor bridle drew
　Until he reached the mound.

Then off there flung in smiling joy,
　And held himself erect
By just his horse's mane, a boy;
　You hardly could suspect
(So tight he kept his lips compressed,
　Scarce any blood came through,)
You looked twice ere you saw his breast
　Was all but shot in two.

" Well, " cried he, " Emperor, by God's grace
　We've got you Ratisbon!
The marshal 's in the market-place,
　And you 'll be there anon
To see your flag-bird flap his vans
　Where I, to heart's desire,
Perched him!" The chief's eye flashed; his plans
　Soared up again like fire.

The chief's eye flashed; but presently
    Softened itself, as sheathes
A film the mother-eagle's eye
    When her bruised eaglet breathes:
" You 're wounded!"   " Nay, " his soldier's pride
    Touched to the quick, he said:
" I 'm killed sire!"   And, his chief beside,
    Smiling, the boy fell dead.

ROBERT BROWNING.

➤✳THE✤HARP✤OF✤TARA✳◄

THE harp that once through Tara's halls
    The soul of music shed,
Now hangs as mute on Tara's walls
    As if that soul were fled.
So sleeps the pride of former days,
    So glory's thrill is o'er,
And hearts that once beat high for praise,
    Now feel that pulse no more.

No more to chiefs and ladies bright
    The harp of Tara swells;
The chord alone that breaks at night
    Its tale of ruin tells.
Thus freedom now so seldom wakes,
    The only throb she gives
Is when some heart indignant breaks
    To show that still she lives.

THOMAS MOORE.

❖FRIENDSHIP❖

A RUDDY drop of manly blood
The surging sea outweighs;
The world uncertain comes and goes,
The lover rooted stays.
I fancied he was fled, —
And, after many a year,
Glowed unexhausted kindliness,
Like daily sunrise there.
My careful heart was free again,
O friend, my bosom said,
Through thee alone the sky is arched,
Through thee the rose is red;
All things through thee take nobler form,
And look beyond the earth;
The mill-round of our fate appears
A sun-path in thy worth.
Me too thy nobleness has taught
To master my despair;
The fountains of my hidden life
Are through thy friendship fair.

RALPH WALDO EMERSON.

❖O❖BREATHE❖NOT❖HIS❖NAME❖

Oh! breathe not his name! let it sleep in the shade,
Where cold and unhonoured his relics are laid;
Sad, silent, and dark be the tears that we shed,
As the night-dew that falls on the grave o'er his head,

But the night dew that falls, though in silence it weeps,
Shall brighten with verdure the grave where he sleeps;
And the tear that we shed, though in secret it rolls,
Shall long keep his memory green in our souls.

THOMAS MOORE.

→❖THE❖PASSIONS❖←

WHEN music, heavenly maid, was young,
While yet in early Greece she sung,
The passions oft, to hear her shell,
Thronged around her magic cell, —
Exulting, trembling, raging, fainting, —
Possessed beyond the muse's painting;
By turns they felt the glowing mind
Disturbed, delighted, raised, refined;
Till once; 't is said, when all were fired,
Filled with fury, rapt, inspired,
From the supporting myrtles round
They snatched her instruments of sound;
And, as they oft had heard apart
Each (for madness ruled the hour)
Would prove his own expressive power.

First Fear his hand, its skill to try,
    Amid the chords bewildered laid,
And back recoiled, he knew not why,
    E'en at the sound himself had made.
Next Anger rushed; his eyes, on fire,
    In lightnings owned his secret stings:
In one rude clash he struck the lyre,
    And swept with hurried hand the strings.

With woful measures wan Despair,
    Low, sullen sounds, his grief beguiled, —
A solemn, strange, and mingled air;
    'T was sad by fits, by starts 't was wild.

But thou, O Hope, with eyes so fair, —
    What was thy delightful measure?
Still it whispered promised pleasure,

And bade the lovely scenes at distance hail!
Still would her touch the strain prolong;
  And from the rocks, the woods, the vale,
She called on Echo still, through all the song;
  And where her sweetest theme she chose,
    A soft responsive voice was heard at every close;
And Hope, enchanted, smiled, and waved her hair.
And longer had she sung—but, with a frown,
  Revenge impatient rose;
He threw his blood-stained sword in thunder down;
  And, with a withering look,
  The war-denouncing trumpet took,
And blew a blast so loud and dread,
Were ne'er prophetic sounds so full of woe!
  And ever and anon he beat
  The doubling drum with furious heat;
And though, sometimes, each dreary pause between,
  Dejected Pity, at his side,
  Her soul-subduing voice applied,
Yet still he kept his wild, unaltered mien,
While each strained ball of sight seemed bursting
  from his head.

Thy numbers, Jealousy, to naught were fixed—
  Sad proof of thy distressful state;
Of differing themes the veering song was mixed;
  And now it courted Love—now, raving, called on
    Hate.

    With eyes upraised, as one inspired,
    Pale Melancholy sate retired;
    And from her wild sequestered seat,
    In notes by distance made more sweet,
Poured through the mellow horn her pensive soul;
    And, dashing soft from rocks around,
    Bubbling runnels joined the sound;
Through glades and glooms the mingled measure
    stole;

Or, o'er some haunted stream, with fond delay,
  Round a holy calm diffusing,
  Love of peace, and lonely musing,
In hollow murmurs died away.

  But oh! how altered was its sprightlier tone
  When Cheerfulness, a nymph of healthiest hue,
Her bow across her shoulder flung,
  Her buskins gemmed with morning dew,
Blew an inspiring air, that dale and thicket rung—
  The hunter's call, to faun and dryad known!
The oak-crowned sisters, and their chaste-eyed queen,
    Satyrs and sylvan boys, were seen,
    Peeping from forth their alleys green;
Brown Exercise rejoiced to hear;
And Sport leapt up, and seized his beechen spear.

Last came Joy's ecstatic trial:
    He, with viny crown advancing,
  First to the lively pipe his hand addrest;
    But soon he saw the brisk awakening viol,
Whose sweet entrancing voice he loved the best:
  They would have thought, who heard the strain,
    They saw, in Tempe's vale, her native maids,
    Amidst the festal-sounding shades,
    To some unwearied minstrel dancing,
    While, as his flying fingers kissed the strings;
Love framed with Mirth a gay fantastic round:
Loose were her tresses seen, her zone unbound,
    And he amidst his frolic play,
    As if he would the charming air repay,
Shook thousand odors from his dewy wings.

  O Music! sphere-descended maid,
  Friend of pleasure, wisdom's aid!
  Why, goddess! why, to us denied,
  Lay'st thou thy ancient lyre aside?
  As, in that loved Athenian bower,

You learned an all-commanding power,
Thy mimic soul, O nymph endeared,
Can well recall what then it heard;
Where is thy native simple heart,
Devote to virtue, fancy, art?
Arise, as in that elder time,
Warm, energetic, chase, sublime!
Thy wonders, in that godlike age,
Fill thy recording sister's page;
'Tis said —and I believe the tale—
Thy humblest reed could more prevail,
Had more of strength, diviner rage
Than all which charms this laggard age—
E'en all at once together found—
Cecilia's mingled world of sound.
Oh bid our vain endeavours cease;
Revive the just designs of Greece!
Return in all thy simple state—
Confirm the tales her sons relate!

WILLIAM COLLINS.

✢LUCY✢

SHE dwelt among the untrodden ways
    Beside the springs of Dove,
A maid whom there was none to praise,
    And very few to love.

A violet by a mossy stone
    Half hidden from the eye!
Fair as a star, when only one
    Is shining in the sky.

She lived unknown, and few could know
    When Lucy ceased to be;
But she is in her grave, and, oh!
    The difference to me.

WILLIAM WORDSWORTH.

→✳MY✢CAPTAIN✳←

O CAPTAIN! my Captain! our fearful trip is done;
The ship has weather'd every rack, the prize we sought is
    won;
The port is near, the bells I hear, the people all exulting,
While follow eyes the steady keel, the vessel grim and
    daring:
        But O heart! heart! heart!
            O the bleeding drops of red,
                Where on the deck my Captain lies,
                    Fallen cold and dead.

O Captain! my Captain! rise up and hear the bells;
Rise up—for you the flag is flung—for you the bugle
    trills;
For you bouquets and ribbon'd wreaths—for you the
    shores a-crowding;
For you they call, the swaying mass, their eager faces
    turning;
        Here Captain! dear father!
            This arm beneath your head;
                It is some dream that on the deck
                    You've fallen cold and dead.

My Captain does not answer, his lips are pale and still;
My father does not feel my arm, he has no pulse nor will:
The ship is anchor'd safe and sound, its voyage closed
    and done;
From fearful trip the victor ship, comes in with object won:
        Exult O shores, and ring, O bells!
            But I, with mournful tread,
                Walk the deck my Captain lies,
                    Fallen cold and dead.

WALT WHITMAN.

SAD IS OUR YOUTH

Sad is our youth, for it ever is going,
Crumbling away beneath our very feet;
Sad is our life, for onward it is flowing
In current unperceived, because so fleet;
Sad are our hopes, for they were sweet in sowing,—
But tares, self sown, have overtopped the wheat;
Sad are our joys, for they were sweet in blowing,—
And still, O, still their dying breath is sweet;
And sweet is youth, although it hath bereft us
Of that which made our childhood sweeter still;
And sweet is middle life, for it hath left us
A nearer good to cure an older ill;
And sweet are all things, when we learn to prize them,
Not for their sake, but His who grants them or denies
   them!

AUBREY DE VERE.

TO OUR LADY

MOTHER! whose virgin bosom was uncrost;
With the least shade of thought to sin allied;
Woman! above all women glorified,
Our tainted nature's solitary boast;
Purer than foam on central ocean tost;
Brighter than eastern skies at daybreak strewn
With fancied roses, than the unblemished moon
Before her wane begins on heaven's blue coast;
Thy Image falls to earth. Yet some, I ween,
Not unforgiven the suppliant knee might bend,
As to a visible Power, in which did blend
All that was mixed and reconciled in thee
Of mother's love with maiden purity,
Of high with low, celestial with terrene!

WILLIAM WORDSWORTH.

SONNET

Shall I compare thee to a Summer's day
Thou art more lovely and more temperate;
Rough winds do shake the darling buds of May,
And Summer's lease hath all to short a date.
Sometimes too hot the eye of heaven shines,
And often is his gold complexion dimmed,
And every fair from fair sometimes declines,
By chance, or nature's changing course, untrimmed;
But thy eternal Summer shall not fade,
Nor lose possession of that fair thou owest;
Nor shall death brag thou wander'st in his shade,
When in eternal lines to time thou growest.
So long as men can breathe, or eyes can see
So long lives this, and this gives life to thee.

WILLIAM SHAKESPEARE.

ECHO AND SILENCE

In eddying course when leaves began to fly,
And Autumn in her lap the store to strew,
Through glens untrod, and woods that frowned on high,
Two sleeping nymphs with wonder mute I spy!
And, lo, she's gone! —In robe of dark-green hue,
'T was Echo from her sister Silence flew,
For quick the hunter's horn resounded to the sky!
In shade affrighted Silence melts away.
Not so her sister.   Hark! for onward still,
With far-heard step, she takes her listening way,
Bounding from rock to rock, and hill to hill.
Ah! mark the merry maid in mockful play
With thousand mimic tones the laughing forest fill!

SIR. SAMUEL EGERTON BRYDGES.

⇥∻BUGLE∻SONG∻⇤

FROM " THE PRINCESS. "

THE splendour falls on castle walls
  And snowy summits old in story;
The long light shakes across the lakes,
  And the wild cataract leaps in glory.
Blow, bugle, blow! set the wild echoes flying;
Blow, bugle; answer, echoes—dying, dying, dying!

O hark! O hear! how thin and clear,
  And thinner, clearer, further going!
O sweet and far, from cliff to scar,
  The horns of Elfland faintly blowing!
Blow, let us hear the purple glens replying;
Blow, bugle; answer, echoes—dying, dying, dying!

O love, they die in yon rich sky;
  They faint on hill or field or river:
Our echoes roll from soul to soul,
  And grow for ever and for ever
Blow, bugle, blow! set the wild echoes flying,
And answer, echoes, answer—dying, dying, dying!

ALFRED TENNYSON.

⇥CHANGE⇤

FROM " TIMES GO BY TURNS. "

Not always fall of leaf, nor even spring,
  Not endless night, nor yet eternal day:
The saddest birds a season find to sing,
  The roughest storm a calm may soon allay.
Thus, with succeeding turns, God tempereth all,
  That man may hope to rise, yet fear to fall.

ROBERT SOUTHWELL, S. J.

⁜ULYSSES⁜

It little profits that, an id'e king,
By this still hearth, among these barren crags,
Matched with an aged wife, I mete and dole
Unequal laws unto a savage race,
That hoard, and sleep, and feed, and know not me.
I cannot rest from travel: I will drink
Life to the lees: all times I have enjoyed
Greatly, have suffered greatly, both with those
That loved me, and alone; on shore, and when
Through scudding drifts the rainy Hyades
Vext the dim sea: I am become a name;
For always roaming with a hungry heart
Much have I seen and known; cities of men
And manners, climates, councils, governments,
Myself not least, but honoured of them all;
And drunk delight of battle with my peers,
Far on the ringing plains of windy Troy.
I am a part of all that I have met;
Yet all experience is an arch wherethrough
Gleams that untraveled world, whose margin fades
Forever and forever when I move.
How dull it is to pause, to make an end,
To rust unburnished, not to shine in use!
As though to breathe were life. Life piled on life
Were all too little, and of one to me
Little remains: but every hour is saved
From the eternal silence, something more,
A bringer of new things; and vile it were
For some three suns to store and hoard myself,
And this gray spirit yearning in desire
To follow knowledge like a sinking star,
Beyond the utmost bound of human thought.

This is my son, mine own Telemachus,
To whom I leave the sceptre and the isle —
Well-loved of me, discerning to fulfil
This labour, by slow prudence to make mild
A rugged people and through soft degrees
Subdue them to the useful and the good.
Most blameless is he, centered in the sphere
Of common duties, decent not to fail
In offices of tenderness, and pay
Meet adoration to my household gods,
When I am gone. He works his work, I mine.
  There lies the port: the vessel puffs her sail:
There gloom the dark broad seas. My mariners,
Souls that have toiled, and wrought, and thought
          with me—
That ever with a frolic welcome took
The thunder and the sunshine, and opposed
Free hearts, free foreheads—you and I are old.
Old age hath yet his honour and his toil;
Death closes all: but something, ere the end,
Some work of noble note, may yet be done,
Not unbecoming men that strove with gods.
The lights begin to twinkle from the rocks:
The long day wanes: the slow moon climbs: the deep
Moans round with many voices. Come my friends,
'Tis not too late to seek a newer world.
Push off, and sitting well in order smite
The surrounding furrows; for my purpose holds
To sail beyond the sunset, and the baths
Of all the western stars, until I die.
It may be that the gulfs will wash us down:
It may be we shall touch the Happy Isles,
And see the great Achilles, whom we knew.
Though much is taken, much abides; and though
We are not now that strength which in old days
Moved earth and heaven; that which we are, we are ;
One equal temper of heroic hearts,

Made weak by time and fate, but strong in will
To strive, to seek, to find, and not to yield.

ALFRED TENNYSON.

❖MEMORY❖

THE mother of muses, we are taught,
Is Memory; she has left me; they remain,
And shake my shoulder, urging me to sing
About the summer days, my loves of old.
" Alas! alas! " is all ⁻can reply,
Memory has left with me that name alone,
Harmonious name, which other bards may sing,
But her bright image in my darkest hour
Comes back, in vain comes back, called or uncalled.
Forgotten are the names of visitors
Ready to press my hand but yesterday;
Forgotten are the names of earlier friends
Whose genial converse and glad countenance
Are fresh as ever to mine ear and eye;
To these, when I have written, and besought
Remembrance of me, the word " Dear " alone
Hangs on the upper verge, and waits in vain.
A blessed wert thou, O Oblivon,
If thy stream carried only weeds away,
But vernal and autumnal flowers alike
It hurries down to wither on the strand.

WALTER SAVAGE LANDOR.

THE STORMY PETREL

A THOUSAND miles from land are we,
Tossing about on the stormy sea—
From billow to bounding billow cast,
Like fleecy snow on the stormy blast.
The sails are scattered abroad like weeds;
The strong masts shake like quivering reeds;
The mighty cables and iron chains,
The hull, which all earthly strength disdains,—
They strain and they crack; and hearts like stone
Their natural, hard, proud strength disown.

Up and down! —up and down!
From the base of the wave to the billow's crown,
And amidst the flashing and feathery foam,
The stormy petrel finds a home—
A home, if such a place may be
For her who lives on the wide, wild sea,
On the craggy ice, in the frozen air,
And only seeketh her rocky lair
To warm her young, and teach them to spring
At once o'er the waves of their stormy wing!

O'er the deep! —o'er the deep!
Where the whale, and the shark, and the sword-fish
      sleep—
Outflying the blast and the driving rain,
The petrel telleth her tale —in vain;
For the mariner curseth the warning bird
Which bringeth him news of the storm unheard.
Ah! thus does the prophet of good or ill
Meet hate from the creatures he serveth still!
Yet he ne'er falters —so, petrel, spring!
Once more o'er the waves on thy stormy wing!

BRYAN W. PROCTOR (*Barry Cornwall.*)

➤❊A❖FORSAKEN❖GARDEN❊◄

In a coign of the cliff between lowland and highland,
　At the sea-down's edge between windward and lee,
Walled round with rocks as an inland island,
　The ghost of a garden fronts the sea.
A girdle of brushwood and thorn encloses
　The steep square slope of the blossomless bed
Where the weeds that grew green from the graves of its
　　roses
　　　　　Now lie dead.

The fields fall southward, abrupt and broken,
　To the low last edge of the long lone land.
If a step should sound or a word be spoken,
　Would a ghost not rise at the strange guest's hand?
So long have the gray bare walks lain guestless,
　Through branches and briers if a man make way,
He shall find no life but the sea-wind's, restless
　　　　　Night and day.

The dense hard passage is blind and stifled
　That crawls by a track none turn to climb
To the strait waste place that the years have rifled
　Of all but the thorns that are touched not of time.
The thorns he spares when the rose is taken;
　The rocks are left when he wastes the plain.
The wind that wanders, the weeds wind-shaken,
　　　　　These remain.

Not a flower to be pressed of the foot that falls not;
　As the heart of a dead man the seed-plots are dry;
From the thicket of thorns whence the nightingale calls
　　not,
Could she call, there were never a rose to reply.

Over the meadows that blossom and wither
Rings but the note of a sea-bird's song;
  Only the sun and the rain come hither
     All year long.

The sun burns sere and the rain dishevels
  One gaunt bleak blossom of scentless breath.
Only the wind here hovers and revels
  In a round where life seems barren as death.
Here there was laughing of old, there was weeping,
  Haply of lovers none ever will know,
Whose eyes went seaward a hundred sleeping
     Years ago.

Heart handfast in heart as they stood, "Look thither,"
  Did he whisper?   "Look forth from the flowers to the
    sea;
For the foam flowers endure when the rose-blossoms
    wither,
  And men that love lightly may die—but we?"
And the same wind sang and the same waves whitened,
  And or ever the garden's last petals were shed,
In the lips that had whispered, the eyes that had light-
    ened,
     Love was dead.

Or they loved their life through, and then went whither?
  And were one to the end—but what end who knows?
Love deep as the sea as a rose must wither,
  As the rose-red seaweed that mocks the rose.
Shall the dead take thought for the dead to love them?
  What love was ever as deep as a grave?
They are loveless now as the grass above them,
     Or the wave.

All are at one now, roses and lovers,
  Not known of the cliffs and the fields and the sea
Not a breath of the time that has been hovers
  In the air now soft with a summer to be.

Not a breath shall there sweeten the seasons hereafter
  Of the flowers or the lovers that laugh now or weep,
When as they that are free now of weeping and laughter
    We shall sleep.

Here death may deal not again for ever;
  Here change may come not till all change end.
From the graves they have made they shall rise up
    never,
  Who have left naught living to ravage and rend.
Earth, stones, and thorns of the wild ground growing,
  While the sun and the rain live, these shall be;
Till a last wind's breath upon all these blowing
    Roll the sea.

Till the slow sea rise and the sheer cliff crumble,
  Till terrace and meadow the deep gulfs drink,
Till the strength of the waves of the high tides humble
  The fields that lessen, the rocks that shrink,
Here now in his triumph where all things falter,
  Stretched out on the spoils that his own hand spread,
As a god self-slain on his own strange altar,
    Death lies dead.
ALGERNON CHARLES SWINBURNE.

→✳FLOWERS✳←

So have I seen, to dress their mistress, May,
Two silken, sister flowers consult, and lay
Their bashful cheeks together: newly they
Peeped from their buds, showed like the garden's eyes
Scarce waked: like was the crimson of their joys;
Like were the pearls they wept; so like, that one
Seemed but the other's kind reflection.
RICHARD CRASHAW.

⸬EPITAPH⸭ON⸭ELIZABETH⸭L⸭H⸭

WOULDST thou hear what man can say
In a little? —reader, stay?
Underneath this stone doth lie
As much beauty as could die—
Which in life did harbour give
To more virtue than doth live.
If at all she had a fault,
Leave it buried in this vault.
One name was Elizabeth —
Th' other, let it sleep with death:
Fitter, where it died to tell,
Than that it lived at all.   Farewell!

BEN JONSON.

⸭TO⸭LUCASTA⸭

ON GOING TO THE WARS.

TELL me not, dear, I am unkind,
  That from the nunnery
Of thy chaste heart and quiet mind,
  To war and arms I flee.

True a new mistress now I chase,
  The first foe in the field;
And with a stronger faith embrace
  A sword, a horse, a shield.

Yet this inconstancy is such
  As you, too, should adore;
I could not love thee, dear, so much,
  Loved I not honour more.

RICHARD LOVELACE.

→❖LOVE'S÷SERVICE❖←

SHE shroudeth vice in virtue's veil,
Pretending good in ill;
She offereth joy, affordeth grief,
A kiss where she doth kill.

A honey-shower rains from her lips,
Sweet lights shine from her face;
She hath the blush of virgin's mind,
The mind of viper's race.

She makes thee seek, yet fear to find,
To find, but not enjoy;
In many frowns some gliding smiles
She yields the more t' annoy.

With soothéd words enthrallèd souls
She chains in servile bands;
Her eye in silence hath a speech
Which eye best understands.

Her little sweet how many sours,
Short hap immortal harms;
Her loving looks are murdering darts,
Her songs bewitching charms.

Her diet is of such delights
As please till they be past;
But then the poison kills the heart
That did entice the taste.

Plough not the seas, sow not the sands,
Leave off your idle pain;
Seek other mistress for your minds;
Love's service is in vain.

ROBERT SOUTHWELL, S. J.

❖HYMN❖BEFORE❖SUNRISE❖

HAST thou a charm to stay the morning-star
In his steep course? So long he seems to pause
On thy bald, awful head, O sovereign Blanc!
The Arve and Arveiron at thy base
Rave ceaselessly ; but thou, most awful Form,
Risest from forth thy silent sea of pines,
How silently! Around thee and above
Deep is the air and dark, substantial, black —
An ebon mass. Methinks thou piercest it,
As with a wedge! But when I look again,
It is thine own calm home,thy crystal shrine,
Thy habitation from eternity!
O dread and silent Mount! I gazed on thee,
Till thou, still present to the bodily sense,
Didst vanish from my thought. Entranced in prayer
I worshipped the invisible alone.
     Yet, like some sweet beguiling melody,
So sweet we know not we are listening to it,
Thou, the meanwhile, wast blending with my thought —
Yea, with my life and life's own secret joy—
Till the dilating soul, enrapt, transfused,
Into the mighty vision passing —there,
As in her natural form, swelled vast to heaven!
     Awake, my soul! not only passive praise
Thou owest! not alone these swelling tears,
Mute thanks and secret ecstasy! Awake,
Voice of sweet song! Awake, my heart, awake!
Green vales and icy cliffs, all join my hymn.
     Thou first and chief, sole sovereign of the vale!
Oh, struggling with the darkness of the night,
And visited all night by troops of stars,
Or when they climb the sky or when they sink --

Companion of the morning-star at dawn,
'Thyself Earth's rosy star, and of the dawn
Co-herald —wake, oh wake, and utter praise!
Who sank thy sunless pillars deep in earth?
Who filled thy countenance with rosy light?
Who made thee parent of perpetual streams?
    And you, ye five wild torrents fiercely glad,
Who called you forth from night and utter death,
From dark and icy caverns called you forth,
Down those precipitous, black, jagged rocks,
For ever shattered and the same for ever?
Who gave you your invulnerable life,
Your strength, your speed, your fury, and your joy,
Unceasing thunder and eternal foam?
And who commanded (and the silence came,)
Here let the billows stiffen, and have rest?
    Ye ice-falls! ye that from the mountain's brow
Adown enormous ravines slope amain —
Torrents, methinks, that heard a mighty voice,
And stopped at once amid their maddest plunge!
Motionless torrents! silent cataracts!
Who made you glorious as the gates of Heaven
Beneath the keen full moon?   Who made the sun
Clothe you with rainbows?   Who, with living flower
Of lovliest blue, spread garlands at your feet?
God!—let the torrents, like a shout of nations,
Answer! and let the ice-plains echo, God!
God! sing ye meadow-streams with gladsome voice!
Ye pine-groves, with your soft and soul-like sounds!
And they too have a voice, yon piles of snow,
And in their perilous fall shall thunder, God!
    Ye living flowers that skirt the eternal frost!
Ye wild goats sporting round the eagle's nest!
Ye eagles, playmates of the mountain-storm!
Ye lightnings, the dread arrows of the clouds!
Ye signs and wonders of the elements!
Utter forth God, and fill the hills with praise!

Thou too, hoar Mount! with thy sky-pointing peaks,
Oft from whose feet the avalanche, unheard,
Shoots downward, glittering through the pure serene,
Into the depth of clouds that veil thy breast—
Thou too again, stupendous Mountain! thou
That as I raise my head, awhile bowed low
In adoration, upward from thy base
Slow travelling with dim eyes suffused with tears,
Solemnly seemest, like a vapory cloud,
To rise before me—Rise, oh ever rise!
Rise like a cloud of incense, from the Earth!
Thou kingly Spirit throned among the hills,
Thou dread ambassador from Earth to Heaven,
Great Hierarch! tell thou the silent sky,
And tell the stars, and tell yon rising sun,
Earth, with her thousand voices, praises God.

SAMUEL TAYLOR COLERIDGE.

→*HOW ✢ SLEEP ✢ THE ✢ BRAVE*←

How sleep the brave, who sink to rest
By all their counts's wishes blest!
When Spring, with dewy fingers cold,
Returns to deck their hallowed mould,
She there shall dress a sweeter sod
Than Fancy's feet have ever trod.

By fairy hands their knell is rung;
By forms unseen their dirge is sung;
There Honour comes, a pilgrim gray,
To bless the turf that wraps their clay;
And Freedom shall awhile repair,
To dwell a weeping hermit there!

WILLIAM COLLINS.

⟶❋ALEXANDER'S❖FEAST❖❋⟵

'Twas at the royal feast, for Persia won
    By Philip's warlike son:
    Aloft in awful state
    The godlike hero sate
    On his imperial throne:
His valiant peers were placed around,
Their brows with roses and with myrtles bound
  (So should desert in arms be crowned;)
The lovely Thais, by his side,
Sate like a blooming Eastern bride
In flower of youth and beauty's pride.
    Happy, happy, happy pair!
      None but the brave,
      None but the brave,
  None but the brave deserves the fair.

Timotheus, placed on high
    Amid the tuneful choir,
    With flying fingers touched the lyre;
The trembling notes ascend the sky,
    And heavenly joys inspire.
The song began by Jove,
Who left his blissful seats above
(Such is the mighty power of love.)
A dragon's fiery form belied the god;
Sublime on radiant spires he rode,
The listening crowd admire the lofty sound,
A present deity! they shout around;
A present deity! the vaulted roofs rebound.
      With ravished ears
      The monarch hears,
      Assumes the god,
      Affects to nod,
  And seems to shake the spheres.

The praise of Bacchus then the sweet musician sung,
  Of Bacchus—ever fair and ever young;
    The jolly god in triumph comes;
    Sound the trumpets; beat the drums:
      Flushed with a purple grace
      He shows his honest face:
Now give the hautboys breath. He comes! he comes!
  Bacchus ever fair and young,
    Drinking joys did first ordain;
  Bacchus' blessings are a treasure,
  Drinking is the soldier's pleasure;
    Rich the treasure,
    Sweet the pleasure,
  Sweet is pleasure after pain.

  Soothed with the sound the king grew vain;
    Fought all his battles o'er again;
And thrice he routed all his foes, and thrice he slew
      the slain.
  The master saw the madness rise;
  His glowing cheeks, his ardent eyes;
  And, while he heaven and earth defied,
  Changed his hand and checked his pride.
    He chose a mournful muse,
    Soft pity to infuse:
  He sung Darius, great and good,
    By too severe a fate,
  Fallen, fallen, fallen, fallen,
  Fallen from his high estate,
    And weltering in his blood;
  Deserted, at his utmost need,
  By those his former bounty fed;
  On the bare earth exposed he lies,
  With not a friend to close his eyes.
With downcast looks the joyless victor sate,
  Revolving in his altered soul
    The various turns of chance below;

And, now and then, a sigh he stole;
And tears began to flow.

Now strike the golden lyre again:
A louder yet, and yet a louder strain.
And rouse him, like a rattling peal of thunder.
   Hark, hark, the horrid sound
    Has raised up his head;
    As awaked from the dead,
   And amazed, he stares around.
Revenge! revenge! Timotheus cries,
  See the furies arise!
 See the snakes that they rear,
 How they hiss in their hair,
And the sparkles that flash from thir eyes!
  Behold a ghastly band,
  Each a torch in his hand!
Those are Grecian ghosts, that in battle were slain,
   And unburied remain,
   Inglorious on the plain:
   Give the vengeance due
   To the valiant crew.
Behold how they toss their torches on high,
 How they point the Persian abodes,
And glittering temples of the hostile gods!
The princes applaud with a furious joy;
And the king seized a flambeau with zeal to destroy:
   Thais led the way,
   To light him to his prey,.
And like another Helen, fired another Troy!
   Thus, long ago,.
  Ere heaving bellows learned to blow,
   While organs yet were mute;
  Timotheus, to his breathing flute,
   And sounding lyre,
Could swell the soul to rage, or kindle soft desire.
 At last divine Cecilia came,

Inventress of the vocal frame;
The sweet enthusiast, from her sacred store,
Enlarged the former narrow bounds,
And added length to solemn sounds,
With nature's mother-wit, and arts unknown before.
Let old Timotheus yield the prise,
Or both divide the crown;
He raised a mortal to the skies,
She drew an angel down.

JOHN DRYDEN.

VIRTUE

Sweet day, so cool, so calm, so bright,
The bridal of the earth and sky!
The dew shall weep thy fall to-night;
For thou must die.

Sweet rose, whose hue, angry and brave,
Bids the rash gazer turn his eye!
Thy root is ever in its grave—
And thou must die.

Sweet spring, full of sweet days and roses,
A box where sweets compacted lie;
Thy music shows ye have your closes,
And all must die.

Only a sweet and virtuous soul,
Like seasoned timber never gives;
But though the whole world turn to coal,
Then chiefly lives.

GEORGE HERBERT.

MY HEART'S IN THE HIGHLANDS

My heart 's in the Highlands, my heart is not here;
My heart 's in the Highlands a-chasing the deer;
Chasing the wild deer, and following the roe,
My heart 's in the Highlands wherever I go.
Farewell to the Highlands, farewell to the North,
The birthplace of valour, the country of worth;
Wherever I wander, wherever I rove,
The hills of the Highlands forever I love.

Farewell to the mountains high covered with snow;
Farewell to the straths and green valleys below;
Farewell to the forests and wild-hanging woods;
Farewell to the torrents and loud-pouring floods.
My heart 's in the Highlands, my heart is not here;
My heart 's in the Highlands a-chasing the deer
Chasing the wild deer, and following the roe,
My heart 's in the Highlands wherever I go.

ROBERT BURNS.

SPRING

Now the lusty spring is seen;
  Golden yellow, gaudy blue,
  Daintily invite the view.
Everywhere, on every green,
Roses blushing as they blow,
  And enticing men to pull;
Lilies whiter than the snow;
  Woodbines of sweet honey full—
All love's emblems, and all cry:
Gather us or we shall die!

BEAUMONT AND FLETCHE .

❖SHE✛WALKS✛IN✛BEAUTY❖

"HEBREW MELODIES."

SHE walks in beauty, like the night
  Of cloudless climes and starry skies,
And all that 's best of dark and bright
  Meet in her aspect and her eyes,
Thus mellowed to that tender light
  Which heaven to gaudy day denies.

One shade the more, one ray the less,
  Had half impaired the nameless grace
Which waves in every raven tress
  Or softly lightens o'er the face,
Where thoughts serenely sweet express
  How pure, how dear their dwelling-place.

And on that cheek and o'er that brow
  So soft, so calm, yet eloquent,
The smiles that win, the tints that glow,
  But tell of days in goodness spent,—
A mind at peace with all below,
  A heart whose love is innocent.

BYRON.

THE VIGIL OF DON INIGO DE LOYOLA

IN THE CHAPEL OF OUR LADY OF MONTSERRAT.

WHEN at thy shrine, most holy maid!
The Spaniard hung his votive blade,
   And bared his helmed brow—
Not that he fear'd war's visage grim,
Or that the battle-field for him
   Had aught to daunt, I trow :

" Glory ! " he cried, " with thee I've done !
Fame ! thy bright theatres I shun,
   To tread fresh pathways now ;
To track thy footsteps, Saviour God !
With throbbing heart, with feet unshod :
   Hear and record my vow.

Yes, THOU shalt reign ! Chain'd to thy throne,
The mind of man thy sway shall own,
   And to its conqueror bow.
Genius his lyre to Thee shall lift,
And intellect its choicest gift
   Proudly on Thee bestow."

Straight on the marble floor he knelt,
And in his breast exulting felt
   A vivid furnace glow ;
Forth to his task the giant sped,
Earth shook abroad beneath his tread,
   And idols were laid low.

India repair'd half Europe's loss :
O'er a new hemisphere the Cross
   Shone in the azure sky ;
And, from the isles of far Japan
To the broad Andes, won o'er man
   A bloodless victory !

FRANCIS MAHONY, FATHER PROUT.

❖RUTH❖

SHE stood breast high amid the corn,
Clasped by the golden light of morn,
Like the sweetheart of the sun,
Who many a glowing kiss had won.

On her cheek an autumn flush
Deeply ripened; such a blush
In the midst of brown was born,
Like red poppies grown with corn.

Round her eyes her tresses fell,
Which were blackest none could tell;
But long lashes veiled a light
That had else been all too bright.

And her hat, with shady brim,
Made her tressy forehead dim.
Thus she stood among the stooks,
Praising God with sweetest looks.

Sure, I said, Heaven did not mean
Where I reap thou shouldst but glean;
Lay thy sheaf adown and come,
Share my harvest and my home.

THOMAS HOOD.

➤✣MY✢NATIVE✢LAND✣⬅

It chanced to me upon a time to sail
  Across the Southern ocean to and fro;
And landing at fair isles, by stream and vale
  Of sensuous blessing did we ofttimes go.
And months of dreamy joys, like joys in sleep,
  Or like a clear, calm stream o'er mossy stone,
Unnoted passed our hearts with voiceless sweep,
  And left us yearning still for lands unknown.

And when found one,—for 't is not hard to find
  In thousand-isled Cathay another isle,—
For one short noon its treasures filled the mind,
  And then again we yearned, and ceased to smile.
And so it was, from isle to isle we passed,
  Like wanton bees or boys on flowers or lips;
And when that all was tasted, then at last
  We thirsted still for draughts instead of sips.

I learned from this there is no Southern land
  Can fill with love the hearts of Northern men.
Sick minds need change; but, when in health they stand
  'Neath foreign skies, their love flies home again.
And thus with me it was : the yearning turned
  From laden airs of cinnamon away,
And stretched far westward, while the full heart burned
  With love for Ireland, looking on Cathay!

My first dear love, all dearer for thy grief!
  My land, that has no peer in all the sea
For verdure, vale, or river, flower or leaf,—
  If first to no man else, thou 'rt first to me.
New loves may come with duties, but the first
  Is deepest yet, —the mother's breath and smiles :
Like that kind face and breast where I was nursed
  Is my poor land, the Niobe of isles.

                                JOHN BOYLE O'REILLY.

A MUSICAL INSTRUMENT

WHAT was he doing, the great god Pan,
    Down in the reeds by the river?
Spreading ruin scattering ban,
Splashing and paddling with hoofs of a goat,
And breaking the golden lilies afloat
    With the dragon-fly on the river?

He tore out a reed, the great god Pan,
    From the deep, cool bed of the river,
The limpid water turbidly ran,
And the broken lilies a-dying lay,
And the dragon-fly had fled away,
    Ere he brought it out of the river.

High on the shore sat the great god Pan,
    While turbidly flowed the river,
And hacked and hewed as a great god can
With his hard, bleak steel at the patient reed,
Till there was not a sign of a leaf indeed
    To prove it fresh from the river.

He cut it short, did the great god Pan,
    (How tall it stood in the river!)
Then drew out the pith like the heart of a man,
Steadily from the outside ring,
Then notched the poor dry empty thing
    In holes, as he sat by the river.

" This is the way," laughed the great god Pan,
    (Laughed while he sate by the river!)
" The only way since gods began
To make sweet music, they could succeed."
Then dropping his mouth to a hole in the reed,
    He blew in power by the river.

Sweet. sweet, sweet, O Pan,
  Piercing sweet by the river!
Blinding sweet, O great god Pan!
The sun on the hill forgot to die,
And the lilies revived, and the dragon-fly
  Came back to dream on the river.

Yet half a beast is the great god Pan,
  To laugh, as he sits by the river,
Making a poet out of a man.
The true gods sigh for the cost and the pain,—
For the reed that grows never more again
  As a reed with the reeds of the river.

ELIZABETH BARRETT BROWNING.

ON FIRST LOOKING INTO CHAPMAN'S HOMER

MUCH have I travelled in the realms of gold,
And many goodly states and kingdoms seen;
Round many western islands have I been
Which bards in fealty to Apollo hold.
Oft of one wide expanse had I been told
That deep-browed Homer ruled as his demesne;
Yet did I never breathe its pure serene
Till I heard Chapman speak out loud and bold:
Then felt I like some watcher of the skies
When a new planet swims into his ken;
Or like stout Cortez, when with eagle eyes
He stared at the Pacific—and his men
Looked at each other with a wild surmise—
Silent, upon a peak in Darien.

JOHN KEATS.

www.ingramcontent.com/pod-product-compliance
Lightning Source LLC
Chambersburg PA
CBHW020406030726
47496CB00007B/2323